CITIZENSHIP ON CATFISH ROW

CITIZENSHIP ON CATFISH ROW

Race and Nation in American Popular Culture

Geoffrey Galt Harpham

THE UNIVERSITY OF
SOUTH CAROLINA PRESS

Published by the University of South Carolina Press
Columbia, South Carolina 29208

www.uscpress.com

Manufactured in the United States of America

31 30 29 28 27 26 25 24 23 22
10 9 8 7 6 5 4 3 2 1

Library of Congress Cataloging-in-Publication Data
can be found at http://catalog.loc.gov/.

ISBN: 978-1-64336-327-1 (hardcover)
ISBN: 978-1-64336-328-8 (paperback)
ISBN: 978-1-64336-329-5 (ebook)

For my children:
Adrian Harpham, Clare Harpham Hall, John Harpham

Contents

INTRODUCTION

Art and America

When they first emerged in something like their modern forms in the eighteenth century, the concepts of race and nation, both loosely defined, did not impinge on each other. The three to five races posited by authorities, all variants of a common human species traceable back to Adam and Eve, were distributed across political boundaries, so that no nation could claim a racial—that is, a genetic or hereditary—identity as its exclusive possession. The first modern nations, the United States and France, announced themselves in universal terms that took no notice of racial differences. This revolutionary affirmation of human solidarity based on the premise that all men are created equal was inscribed into the Declaration of Independence, which continues to have legal force in the United States despite that it was written before there was a nation to legitimate it.

A few years after the 1776 Revolution but a few years before the ratification of the Constitution, Thomas Jefferson, the author of the phrase about universal human equality, was assigned the task of replying to questions about his home state posed by a French diplomat. He took the opportunity to produce what became his only book, *Notes on the State of Virginia*,[1] an exhaustive survey of the climate, topography, commerce, educational

1. Thomas Jefferson, *Notes on the State of Virginia* (Boston: Lilly and Wait, 1832), https://tile.loc.gov/storage-services/service/gdc/lhbcb/04902/04902.pdf.

institutions, administrative structure, religion, manners, and laws of Virginia, with many extensions of his analysis to the entire country. Begun under highly stressed circumstances, with Jefferson, who had just lost a daughter to illness, having fled Monticello to avoid capture by General Cornwallis, *Notes* is a remarkable inventory, displaying an extraordinary command of details as well as an assured grasp of complex patterns, tendencies, potentialities, and general principles. Today, however, the book is most often read for Jefferson's reflections on race. These reflections, so oddly distended and tonally discordant with the administrative neutrality of the rest of the book, expose Jefferson to charges of personal racism, but as scholar Winthrop Jordan notes, the failing is not merely personal, for Jefferson's "enormous breadth of interest and his lack of originality make him an effective sounding board for his culture."[2]

Like the scientific community of the time, the culture Jefferson represented was deeply uncertain about the concept of race, and especially about the origin of racial differences. Both a revolutionary and a man "immensely capable of placid receptivity," as Jordan says, Jefferson deplored slavery but held slaves (431). Considering Virginia, and the nation as seen through the lens of Virginia, Jefferson tried to find a way through the thicket of contradictions in which he was enmeshed, describing Negroes as both indisputably among the creatures of God and therefore worthy of the inherent and inalienable rights enjoyed by all humans, and at the same time as inferior to whites and even to Indians, and therefore, in some sense or degree excluded from the community of rights-bearing humans.

Jefferson was particularly interested in what he saw as the biologically determined differences between whites and Negroes —differences of appearance, of course, but also behavior, moral

2. Winthrop D. Jordan, *White Over Black: American Attitudes toward the Negro, 1550–1812*, 2nd ed. (Chapel Hill: University of North Carolina Press, 2012), 429.

character, and mental capacity. Negroes were, he wrote, capable of bravery, had good memories, and were able to "imagine a small catch" of music (147). But, burdened by imaginations that were "wild and extravagant [escaping] incessantly from every restraint of reason and taste [leaving] a tract of thought as incoherent and eccentric, as is the course of a meteor through the sky," they were "much inferior" in point of reasoning (147). Virtually none was capable of grasping Euclid, and despite the wild extravagance of their imaginations, they were also "dull, tasteless, and anomalous" with respect to--imagination (146). They slept more than whites and lived more in their senses than in their minds. Negro men were "more ardent after their female" than whites despite the fact that the females who excited that ardor were decidedly less beautiful than white women because while white faces had an appealing combination of white and red that varied as the emotion dictated, an "eternal monotony . . . an immovable veil of black" covered all the emotions of Negroes (144–45).

Taken all together, these differences, coupled with others recently determined by science about respiration and kidney secretion, might, Jefferson suggested, indicate something approaching a species difference that could almost justify or at least begin to explain how one race could enslave another even while professing a belief in universal rights: as Jefferson noted, it was "nature which has produced the distinction" (149). Jordan describes the entire passage from which I have quoted—taken from the section on "Laws"—as "intellectual wreckage," pointing in particular to the "geyser of libidinal energy" that gushed forth as the habitually restrained Jefferson considered the questions of beauty and sexuality (453, 458).

By this route we arrive at the subject of this book, the connection between nation and race in America. Popular culture, the category in which I place the three works that organize this discussion, more or less celebrates intellectual wreckage and is altogether given over to geysers of libidinal energy. This orientation, or disorientation, I will argue, gives popular culture an advantage over Enlightenment political philosophy in representing the American character. Untroubled by contradictions or gaps between principles and practices, artists such as Edna Ferber, George Gershwin, Oscar Hammerstein, DuBose Heyward, D. W. Griffith, and even Thomas Dixon, author of the novel on which *The Birth of a Nation* was based, could see some things more clearly than the farsighted Jefferson. Unburdened by the practical, philosophical, economic, political, or moral considerations that so troubled Jefferson, and also by some of his limitations of sympathy or experience, these artists, all working in the Jim Crow era, were actually more capable than Jefferson of undertaking a project he never considered: the creation not of the nation but of a narrative of the nation.

The three astonishing and radically innovative works taken up in this book—the first great narrative film, D. W. Griffith's *The Birth of a Nation* (1915); the first "integrated" musical, Jerome Kern and Oscar Hammerstein's *Show Boat* (1936); and the first great American opera, or "folk-opera," George Gershwin's *Porgy and Bess* (1935)—all have foundational status in their respective genres. Among the very greatest and historically most important works of their kind, they are not unambitious as works of art, but they would never be mistaken for instances of systematic reflection on the issues they raise, and I make no claim for their creators as intellectuals or theorists. And yet, the artistic power these works possess radiates outward to their entire fields of reference, warming and illuminating it all, even if not directly or thoroughly, and even, apparently, without anything that could be considered a fully conscious or focused authorial intention. They are all collectively produced works intended to reach a large audience, an unknown, still-to-be recruited mass of people whom the works address or, more precisely, solicit, not as questers after enlightenment, seekers of the truth, or responsible citizens in a just society, but as consumers of mass entertainment who want to leave the theater refreshed, uplifted, invigorated, and satisfied, with a light heart and a clean conscience.

Shallowness has its own form of depth, and one of the little miracles of art, especially fictional narrative, is the way in which a work that excites in an audience this primitive psychic state can also engage more difficult issues through allusion, implication, or indirection. The conscience of the king, as Hamlet understood, can be caught by an actor doing what King Claudius in fact did—pouring poison into a king's ear as he slept—but it can also be caught by the king's perception of some affinity between what he sees on the stage and something he did, thought about doing, secretly wanted to do, imagined doing, or simply imagined. So hungry is the mind for traces of itself that it can make food of almost anything. A Claudius who was as imaginative as he was guilty might see the finger of accusation pointing at him while watching a hummingbird, a child pinching the head off a dandelion, someone looking through a keyhole, a trumpet player, a maid pouring milk into a bowl, a man cupping his ear and saying "What?"—anything at all. Narrative fiction offers itself to its audience as exemplary but declines to say what it is an example of, which leaves it to the audience.

Fictional narrative provides countless opportunities to raise subjects whose true center or real import is elsewhere or other. Something—the distant source of someone's wealth, for example—might be mentioned without emphasis or comment but the attentive and informed reader of Jane Austen's *Mansfield Park* could recognize that Sir Thomas Bertram's ownership of a slave plantation in Antigua connects the economy that enables these attractive young people to concern themselves with flirtations, betrayals, and courtships to a larger unmentioned horror. A mere figure of speech tossed off by a character or narrator can reveal an energy or an interest that for some undisclosed reason has become detached from literal expression and has secreted itself in an apparently meaningless or innocent bit of rhetoric. Every detail suggests a class, every nuance an argument, every incident a pattern, all of which are left to the audience to assemble as they will, or will not. A single butler can suggest butlers in general, service in general, deference in general, class distinctions in general, *The Remains of the Day* in general, or Britain in general. In this way narrative fiction can trouble the mind with a sense of something disappearing around the corner, just out of focus, something just below the surface that may mean something . . . meanwhile, the narrative, with its insistent particularities, has moved on.

Works of art that come to be considered "major," "great," or "canonical" are those that can be shown to operate at multiple levels, with a surface appealing enough to engage the attention but with a suggestion of other forces that are not directly registered. These other strata emerge into visibility only under the pressure of an analysis that undertakes to realize the potentialities created by the work by assembling hints and signals into patterns that suggest a different design, a different field of reference, a different kind of subject from the one we see on the page, stage, or screen. The sense of a positive relation between levels or types of meaning creates a new kind of interest and a new total conception of the work, more chord or counterpoint than single note or melody. This is the kind of argument I am making for these three works: one reason they must be considered major works of art is that, often without seeming fully aware, they possess this layered or palimpsestic quality, with patterns of implication resonating at different frequencies, each level interfering with, commenting on, or serving as a proxy for others, creating complex harmonies or dissonances we must cup our ears to hear.

The striking and deeply suggestive fact around which this inquiry is organized is that these three very different works share a common ambition. Each one launches an entire genre with a radically innovative work that attempts to represent the character, essence, spirit, or national identity of America in narrative form. Narrative is the privileged bearer of culture and heritage, and all nations tell stories about themselves. But as a nation that invented itself in full view of the world, conceived of itself as an unprecedented new beginning, and installed the concept of the search for a more perfect union at the center of national self-understanding, America has always had a particularly strong narrative character, a fact that has lent a certain urgency to the search for the great American novel. The literary scholar Andrew Delbanco begins his meditation on *The Real American Dream: A Meditation on Hope* with a salute to narrative, which alone, he says, can help us "navigate through life."[3] Hope is the one constant in American history, Delbanco says, but in his account, the object of hope has been shrinking steadily since the Puritans, passing through protracted phases of "God" and "Nation" before coming to rest, at least in the late 1990s when he was writing, on the (to him) sadly diminished and morally unworthy "Self." This steady declension over the centuries notwithstanding, Delbanco, still buoyantly American, holds out the prospect for a new, more expansive phase in which Americans grow weary of self and begin to look outward, translating the American dream into a "global dream." He invokes a bedrock "civil religion," and points out that "against all odds, the live issues of our day are still sometimes debated with dignity" (112).

In the years since that sentence was written, dignity has been subjected to an undignified battering, but one wonders about the adequacy of any account that does not include the experience of those who have not had the luxury of passing through phases of hope, who for much of their long history have had have had little reason to hope for much from the world at all, and for whom the concepts of God, nation, and self, not to mention the world, do not have the same meaning or value as

3. Andrew Delbanco, *The Real American Dream: A Meditation on Hope* (Cambridge, MA: Harvard University Press, 2000), 1.

they do for those aspirational Americans Delbanco talks about. For Delbanco—and for theorists of many persuasions—the United States is an egalitarian democracy that includes some flaws, discrepancies, contradictions, and exclusions that will eventually yield to enlightenment or social pressure and, in due course, disappear. America is large, it contains multitudes, but the civic cacophony will, such theorists maintain, eventually be resolved into unity as the commitment to freedom all Americans have implicitly made is gradually realized in practice.

At the level of theory, such sentiments may be tenable, but they do not describe the actual history of the nation, much of which has borne witness to a series of silent or unmarked exceptions to the Declaration's assertion of universal equality. This brings us to a second point about the three works discussed here: in their effort to tell, and to sell, the American story, they all include an element that may have seemed to their creators a deviation from the main point or marginal to the broader theme they were trying to communicate. This is the subject of race.

It may be surprising or even perversely counterintuitive to describe race in *The Birth of a Nation* as secondary to the main concern of a film that seems from a contemporary perspective to be obsessed with the subject. The film begins with the arrival of the first black slaves, who are identified as impediments to the unity of the nation-to-be—"seeds of disunion" whose massively destructive flowering the film proceeds to document. To many early viewers, and to virtually all in recent decades, race is Griffith's primary subject, and the film as a whole amounts to an appalling disclosure of his personal racism made all the more appalling by the fact that that it is presented as a triumphant and uncontroversial boast. The argument explored here is that the film is more productively seen as centered on the theme of the birth of a nation, and that Griffith's treatment of race is more thoughtless than evil. The absence of thought can be a deeply revealing kind of thought, and the film becomes, I will argue, a more challenging and probing document when seen not just as a racist tract but also as an attempt to tell the story of the nation without having bothered fully to understand the role of race in that story.

Such negligence cannot be attributed to Thomas Dixon, the complex, combative, and darkly gifted figure who wrote the 1905 novel *The Clansman,* on which Griffith's film was based. The powerful influence over the film of Dixon, who both does and does not live up to the conventional image of the bloody-minded Klan-supporting Southern racist constitutes another level of depth in Griffith's great film, which translated an ideology that spoke to a large but still limited number of people into entertainment that addressed a far larger and less homogeneous audience. Whatever else Griffith's film is, it is simple and direct in its portrayal of history. Simplicity and directness are often accounted virtues, and this may help explain the otherwise puzzling respect that several recent black filmmakers have for *The Birth of a Nation.*

For contemporary audiences Griffith's film has a decidedly archaic quality, and seems a monstrous shambling survival from a premodern, if not prehistorical, era. Jerome Kern and Oscar Hammerstein's 1936 film *Show Boat,* based on Edna Ferber's 1925 novel of the same name, speaks a language more readily understandable to a culture long familiar with cinematic entertainment. Griffith had serious ambitions for film as a source of historical knowledge and moral instruction for the masses, but Kern and Hammerstein were interested in film as entertainment and the history of entertainment, and created in *Show Boat* a glittering chronicle of forty years of American show business, beginning on the Mississippi River in the 1880s and extending all the way to Broadway in the 1920s. Between the 1925 novel and the 1936 film, the property actually passed through a chrysalis phase as a Florenz Ziegfeld production. An anomaly in the Ziegfeld oeuvre because of its serious, respectful, and compassionate treatment of race in some early scenes, this production served as the basis for Hammerstein's film, which, however, introduced an extended blackface sequence that removed a good deal of that seriousness; and then, in the film's second half, the entire subject was effectively forgotten, so that race seemed at most a "strain," as one critic put it, within a larger composition. I argue here that race never really vanishes because the strain arising from race drives the entire plot, including and in fact most decisively the parts where the issue does not appear. In effect, I argue that the forgetting of race is the real subject of the film. *Show Boat* is often praised as the pioneer in the integration of musical elements with character and plot, as well as the integration of black and white characters. It has also been praised for its bold and unflinching allusions to the complex realities of race in the South at the end of the nineteenth century. But the brevity of the allusions, and their inclusion in a work so manifestly devoted to gaiety and so relentlessly driving towards an exuberantly happy ending, suggests either an untroubled pseudo-concern on the part of the creators, who may have felt that their responsibilities had been discharged with a mention or, perhaps, a more biting indictment of audiences who were capable of considering as mere entertainment a work that includes such a mention, and then permits the subject to disappear without a trace.

Appearing for the first time a year before the film version of *Show Boat,* but revived periodically, Gershwin's opera speaks to us even more directly. The language it speaks, or sings, is at the core of the controversies that have always surrounded the work. A smoothed-out version of the already smoothed-out version of the Gullah dialect represented in DuBose Heyward's 1925 novel *Porgy,* the language of the opera has always drawn criticism as an implied insult to black people generally. In Heyward's novel, which has the same deep and determining relationship to Gershwin's opera that Dixon's to *Birth of a Nation* and Ferber's to *Show Boat,* Gullah speech is represented more nearly as Heyward heard it. He heard it so early and often that his biographer actually speculates it may have been his first language. In his novel Heyward tried to represent the speech of working people who had little knowledge of the world, were minimally literate, knew one another well, had a common history going back to Africa, and who in general had few worldly aspirations from the present. This was not the position or the condition of most black people in the country—certainly not of the "talented tenth" celebrated by W. E. B. Du Bois. And with each passing year, the sense that the work is offensive to the larger group has grown closer to a consensus. It has for many decades been difficult even for critics or audiences who can appreciate Gershwin's musical achievement to see the opera as something other than a disturbing or problematic representation of black people. Almost every production after the first has introduced modifications intended to bring the opera into closer alignment with contemporary views and values. But the controversy remains, along with the suspicion that the opera, apart from its status as a piece of music, is in the end only a white man's version of black people, which must be flawed and therefore must be corrected if not repudiated. I try here to reorient the understanding of this work and reintroduce it as a live subject for contemporary reflection, by arguing that a more radical and challenging reading would begin with the premise that the Gullah people represented in the opera should be seen not only as representative African Americans but also as proxies for all those who came to America, and that citizenship not race is the real subject.

No single factor accounts for the role of race in these three works. Having grown up in the post-Reconstruction South, where versions of Dixon's story of the heroic rise of the Ku Klux Klan were told in countless (white) households, Griffith saw *The Clansman* as a vehicle for his vast cinematic ambition—a big story involving strong, simple emotions and stirring scenes of action, some involving horses and guns. For Hammerstein the incidents involving black people in *Show Boat* were part of his source material, and given the often-asserted musicality of black people—as it turned out, they were capable of doing more than "imagining a small catch" of music—lent themselves well to musical theater. Gershwin, who determined early on that he wanted to create a specifically American music, was, like many others, drawn to the work of black musicians, many of whom he knew well. None of the people involved in the creation of these works could be called politically or socially radical. None was an activist for change. Still Griffith, Hammerstein, and Gershwin each regarded the work in question as the most important he had ever attempted, and each committed himself to material that included the prominent representation of black people.

They chose this material despite that it created extraordinary problems for their works, and for them. Griffith concludes his epic film with scenes of black people being pursued and shot by scores of mounted Klansmen, followed by a scene in which armed Klansmen prevent black people (a majority of voting-age citizens in South Carolina) from voting. This scene, the most literal possible illustration of what Charles W. Mills calls "*Herrenvolk* [master race] democracy" in which the fine egalitarianism of the nation's official ideology reveals itself as a "racial polity," gives way to a sequence showing the seaside honeymoons of two white couples; this, in turn, is followed by a ghostly, outsized image of Christ presiding serenely over a festive crowd of beautiful young (white, indeed bleached) people, followed by a concluding message, a quotation from Daniel Webster: "Liberty and union, one and inseparable, now and forever." What can Griffith have been thinking—what about all those guns, all those bodies, all that terror in the streets? He could not have known at the time what he later learned, that this film would mark the apogee of his career and the point at which his reputation began its descent, his masterwork becoming in time the most despised artifact ever produced in the United States.

Hammerstein's generally lighthearted and often sentimental musical also creates problems for itself by its inclusion of racial issues. The inspiring performance by Paul Robeson of "Ol' Man River" and the subsequent scene in which a bi-racial woman, exposed for having passed as white, is thrown out into an unforgiving world make the rest of this long film seem anti-climactic and frivolous by comparison and the entire film out of phase with itself, its end forgetful of its beginning. As for *Porgy and Bess,* the Creole character of the Gullah dialect—delightful, amusing, and musical to white ears—bespeaks not only a singular cultural heritage but also to the isolation and exclusion of these people from the American mainstream. No aria, however magnificent or moving, can fully efface the many forms of dispossession entailed by that exclusion, although it seems to many critics that such aestheticizing erasure is part of the intention. The reputations of the opera and of Gershwin himself have suffered because of the suspicion that the entirety is not an assertion of the human dignity of dispossessed and marginalized people, but a testament to, and example of, unwitting prejudice and ignorance.

In all three works, race represents a discordant or disharmonious element—a point of "disunion"—that subverts the coherence and complicates the reception of the work in ways that could have been foreseen. If the creators nevertheless focused on race, they must have felt that the American story they wanted to tell demanded it, and that an avoidance of race would have violated some principle more important than coherence, more important even than public acclaim or critical appreciation, and that the risk therefore had to be run.

To the first two points of consensus among these artists mentioned earlier—telling the American story and focusing on the issue of race—we must then add a third. Griffith, Hammerstein, and Gershwin each discovered, even if he did not fully realize it, that the factor of race made it impossible to tell a coherent linear story about America. The nation had never identified, and had often vigorously denied that it needed or even wanted, a large enveloping concept that might gather together and organize all its forces and energies into a perfectly resolved and harmonious aesthetic form, much less a perfect union. As entertainment their works were under no obligation to eliminate inconsistencies or address all relevant conceptual difficulties. Popular entertainment is not theory, and its mission is not to challenge or accuse. Like the novelists whose works they adapted, Griffith, Hammerstein, and Gershwin all made peace with the limitations in their material and did not attempt a new narrative synthesis that might tell the national story in a more comprehensive and accurate way. But the irresponsibility in telling that story that marks their works as historically, socially, or morally unserious permitted a remarkable candor and directness that, even with the passage of time, retains the power to disturb and —the more difficult recognition—to instruct.

Extracting, articulating, and developing the implications of that instruction so that these works can be reintroduced into a national conversation urgently in need of fresh thinking and cultural memory is the task of this book.

1

THE NATION IN *THE BIRTH OF A NATION*

> Now I could see a chance to do this ride-to-the-rescue on a grand scale. Instead of saving one poor little Nell of the Plains, this ride would be to save a nation.
>
> —*D. W. Griffith*[1]

For a film routinely described as the most controversial motion picture of all time, D. W. Griffith's 1915 *The Birth of a Nation* has excited very little actual disagreement. An immense mass of scholarly research and critical commentary—surely more than that devoted to any film with the exception of *Citizen Kane*—has settled into a solid consensus on two views that exist in quivering tension, neither complementing nor negating the other.

First, Griffith's three-hour epic represents the most important event in the early history of the medium, marking a sudden advance in terms of cinematic technique and narrative ambition over previous films, mostly one-reel nickelodeon entertainments shown in small theaters. So extraordinary and decisive was the break from previous practice that Griffith seemed almost to have invented cinema itself. On his death in 1948, James Agee described him as a "primitive tribal poet," the most consequential

1. D. W. Griffith, "The Hollywood Gold Rush," as told to Jim Hart, in *The Man Who Invented Hollywood: The Autobiography of D. W. Griffith*, ed. and annotated by James Hart (Louisville, KY: Touchstone Publishing Company, 1972), 89.

figure in the history of film. "To watch his work," Agee wrote, "is like being witness to the beginning of melody, or the first conscious use of the lever or the wheel . . . the birth of an art."[2] In the course of creating modern cinematic narrative realism, Griffith introduced naturalistic acting to film and also created the concept of the director as a masterly creative force equal in stature to a composer, an author, a painter. Accompanied by a musical score played in large, big-city theaters by a live symphony orchestra, his masterpiece was seen by far more people, and created far more public discussion, than any previous film, becoming one of the first instances of mass entertainment serving as an instrument for shaping public opinion and even national self-understanding, and one of the first that could qualify as what Griffith called "a moral and educational force."[3] Originally titled *The Clansman*,[4] the title of the 1905 novel by Thomas Dixon, Jr. on which the second half of the film was primarily based, *The Birth of a Nation* was re-titled, according to an often-repeated story, by Dixon himself, who shouted out the suggestion

2. James Agee, "David Wark Griffith," *Agee on Film: Criticism and Comment on the Movies* (New York: Modern Library, 2000), 314,; Ibid. 311. For a detailed account of the many technical innovations involved in Griffith's transformation of the medium "from a cinema of attractions to one based on narrative integration," see Tom Gunning, *D. W. Griffith and the Origins of American Narrative Film: The Early Years at Biograph* (Urbana and Chicago: University of Illinois Press, 1991), 35.

3. D. W. Griffith, quoted in an interview titled "D. W. Griffith, Producer of the World's Biggest Picture," *New York American*, 28 February 1915; in Harry M. Geduld, ed., *Focus on D. W. Griffith* (Englewood Cliffs, NJ: Prentice-Hall, 1971), 27–29. A strong claim to being the very first instance of American mass entertainment to serve as ideological and moral force could be made for Harriet Beecher Stowe's 1852 *Uncle Tom's Cabin* and the countless stage versions it inspired, as well as the half-dozen or so film versions produced between 1903 and 1927.

4. Thomas Dixon Jr., *The Clansman: An Historical Romance of the Ku Klux Klan* (Lexington: University Press of Kentucky, 1970).

to Griffith from the balcony after seeing the film for the first time. The new title invited audiences to understand the story not as a narrative of events happening to a few people in Piedmont, South Carolina but as an allegory for national emergence. By providing what one critic has described as "a template for the vast, world-embracing capabilities of the cinema,"[5] *Birth of a Nation* opened up the medium to virtuosity and ambition. One might say that Griffith made cinema safe for genius. Michael Rogin is not alone in calling the film "the single most important movie ever made."[6]

The second point of consensus is that *Birth of a Nation* is the most despicable major artifact ever produced in the United States. Celebrating the Old South and glorifying the New South as represented by the rise of the Ku Klux Klan, the film misrepresents history, retails stereotypes of African Americans, and praises the killing of black people by the Klan as a form of heroism. The film makes its case by presenting an inventory of clichés and slurs: scenes of slave life in which music and dancing play a leading role; fond portrayals of "faithful souls" loyal to their former masters after the war; exaggerated depictions of Negro legislators installed through the radical Reconstruction regime, shoeless, drunk, lewd, and generally failing to take their governance responsibilities seriously; historically inaccurate scenes of armed black soldiers vandalizing the homes of terrified white citizens; and worst of all, a long scene in which a black man pursues a terrified young white woman who leaps to her death rather than submit to his foul embrace. All this is followed by the climactic episode in which the riders of the Klan race, to the

5. Richard Brody, "The Worst Thing about 'Birth of a Nation' is How Good it is," *New Yorker*, February 1, 2013, https://www.newyorker.com/culture/richard-brody/the-worst-thing-about-birth-of-a-nation-is-how-good-it-is.

6. Michael Rogin, *Blackface, White Noise: Jewish Immigrants in the Hollywood Melting Pot* (Berkeley: University of California Press, 1996), 14.

accompaniment of "The Ride of the Valkyries," to avenge her death and rescue other whites from black marauders. The film not only legitimates but, with a ghastly candor, glorifies attitudes and acts of which a majority of the nation has long been ashamed, documenting, celebrating, and reanimating a pestilential legacy of slavery and racial hatred. Before opening fire in a Charleston, South Carolina church in 2016, a mass murderer provided one of his nine black victims with an explanation that might have come out of the mouth of "The Little Colonel" Ben Cameron, leader of the Klan in Griffith's film: "I have to do this because you are raping our women and taking over the world."

And there the matter stands. As a moment in the history —especially the American history—of the cinematic medium, Griffith's film must be praised in the highest terms; but as an expression of a particular American worldview, it must be condemned in the harshest terms. *The Birth of a Nation* represents the most extreme possible form of the aporia on display in the works of many ideologically or morally suspect artists whose formal or technical achievements compel a grudging and limited respect from those who deplore both content and creator. In Griffith's case, critical thought is particularly frozen, and must, it seems, remain so as long as the film is seen as an unequivocal and unembarrassed endorsement of white supremacy and racial violence. In an era when racism has become a term for radical evil, anything to which the term sticks, as it certainly has to *Birth of a Nation* and its creators, has no rejoinder. It has become all but impossible to discuss the film without encasing the discussion in a moral judgment. Understanding begins in shame and outrage, and critics seem to vie with one other in a holy contest to see who can devise the most vehement expressions of personal revulsion at what Griffith has wrought.

But to condemn *Birth of a Nation* as the work of one or two wicked people is to seek false comfort in a distant and localized evil, and to miss an opportunity for new insight. In the beliefs that an artifact of this stature in both the history of cinema and the history of the nation ought to be the subject of ongoing reflection, and that reflection—by which I mean a kind of provisional acceptance of the possibility that even the America of the twenty-first century is somehow, in some way, registered or reflected in the film—ought not to be suffocated by moral or political commitments, I would like to approach *Birth of a Nation* from a different perspective. I do not question the inescapability of race in any discussion, but simply wish to recast the discussion, beginning with the fact that many politically and socially progressive viewers who clearly feel they should be deeply disturbed—who actually want to be disturbed—by the experience of seeing it are not, or not only.[7] The explanation cannot be merely that the rescue of a damsel in distress is universally thrilling. There are other damsels in other films—a great many of them by Griffith; it was his recurrent theme—that do not stick in, much less trouble the mind. There must be something deeper and more complex at stake. That thing, I will argue, is hiding in plain sight. It is the concept of the American nation, rendered by Griffith with a brutal clarity.

Evidence that the film was always felt to have national rather than purely artistic or cinematic stakes is provided by one of the most striking aspects of its reception, the often-voiced conviction that the film is a deadly cultural virus and should not be merely critiqued or regulated but banned altogether lest it corrupt the body politic. This conviction has been present from the very beginning, when the NAACP—at that time a small, underfunded organization founded seven years before by W. E. B. Du Bois and others who had been concerned with such issues

7. As Richard Brody says, "The worst thing about 'Birth of a Nation' is how good it is. The merits of its grand and enduring aesthetic make it impossible to ignore and, despite its disgusting content, also make it hard not to love. And it's that very conflict that renders the film all the more despicable, the experience of the film more of a torment." Brody, "The Worst Thing."

as housing segregation or lynchings—undertook a coordinated multi-city campaign to censor, and, when that failed, to suppress the film, which also failed.[8] Adopting the tone of the high-minded artist concerned about free expression and artistic integrity, Griffith fought and mostly defeated these efforts in the courts, the newspapers, and the local censorship boards, but the critics were so numerous and their case so compelling that he eventually came to agree with them. Interviewed in 1941 when he was unemployed and living alone in a small apartment near Hollywood and Vine, he said that only film students should be permitted to see it because "the Negro race has had enough trouble, more than enough of its share of injustice, oppression, tragedy, suffering, and sorrow."[9] His generous thoughts did not save him: in 1996, he himself was suppressed when his

8. On the NAACP campaign against the film in various cities, see Melvyn Stokes, *D. W. Griffith's* The Birth of a Nation: *A History of "The Most Controversial Motion Picture of all Time,"* (New York: Oxford University Press, 2007), 129–70, and 227–75. See also Stephen Weinberger, "The Birth of a Nation and the Making of the NAACP" *Journal of American Studies*, 45 (February 2011) 1: 77–93. For an account of the Boston-based opposition led by William Monroe Trotter, see *The Birth of a Movement,* directed by Susan Gray and Bestor Cram (PBS, 2017). http://www.pbs.org/independentlens/videos/birth-movement-trailer/. For a more comprehensive discussion, see Nickiann Fleener-Marzec, *D. W. Griffith's* The Birth of a Nation*: Controversy, Suppression, and the First Amendment as it Applies to Filmic Expression, 1915–73* (New York: Arno Press, 1980). For Griffith's own contribution to this debate, see David Wark Griffith, "The Rise and Fall of Free Speech in America," (Los Angeles, CA, n.p., 1916), http://filmstudies.info/consulted/texts/The_Rise_and_Fall_of_Free_Speech_in_Amer.pdf.

9. Griffith to biographer Barnet Bravermann, recorded in an unpublished MS cited in Ira H. Gallen, *D. W. Griffith Master of Cinema* (Victoria, BC: Friesen Press, 2015), 491. On Griffith's last years, see Richard Schickel, *D. W. Griffith: An American Life* (New York: Proscenium, 1996), 560–605; and Richard Batman, "D. W. Griffith: The Lean Years," *California Historical Society Quarterly* 44, no. 3 (Sep. 1965): 195–204.

name was removed from the Lifetime Achievement Award given by the Director's Guild. Now rarely screened, the film retains its toxicity, which extends to anyone or anything associated with it.[10]

Cinema is viral by nature, but Griffith's film takes virality as its main theme, describing the birth of the nation as a series of actions that appear at first to be limited and rational but are then taken over by some malign inner mechanism of self-replication. The Civil War begins, in the film, with the feel-good attack on Fort Sumter, which prompts gallant sons of the South to enlist in the noble cause; but then, after an easy Confederate victory at Bull Run, the conflict rapidly engulfs the entire nation and ends after four years of slaughter with the utter defeat and destruction of the South and the assassination of President Lincoln. Reconstruction then begins as an attempt to reintegrate the South into the Union, that, driven by the vengeful fanatic Austin Stoneman—modeled on Senator Thaddeus Stevens of Pennsylvania—almost immediately mutates into a program of humiliation and oppression that threatens the destruction of everything the war had not already destroyed. The Ku Klux Klan, formed as a citizen's response to Negro assaults on innocent white people, instantly becomes, in the words of Dixon's novel, a "gale of chivalrous passion and high action, contagious and intoxicating" that "swept the white race" (*Clansman,* 341). In 1871–72, the United States Congress, alarmed by the violence unleashed by the Klan in "the late insurrectionary states," held hearings the record of which filled thirteen volumes including thousands of pages of first-hand testimony that gave the public a sense of the

10. To take just two recent examples: in Spring 2019 an original poster for the film became the object of student protests at Chapman University in Los Angeles; at the same time, the trustees of Bowling Green University removed the names of Lillian and Dorothy Gish from the campus theater the sisters had helped to build, citing student distress at the presence of the Gish name on campus—Lillian (but not Dorothy) had appeared in the film. The endowment gift was of course retained.

shape this chivalry had taken.[11] By 1915, when Griffith's film was released, the public had also learned of hundreds of lynchings and other forms of murder and violence over the previous two decades. With the inspiration provided by the film, a "second Klan" emerged at this time, this one not confined to the South, and it became possible to see programmatic racial violence as another instance of an impulse that had begun, long ago, in a few locations, on a modest scale for reasons that some people at a certain time and place had found necessary and even honorable, but that had spun wildly out of control and now threatened to infect the mainstream of American society.[12]

One could, then, describe the nation whose birth is chronicled in, and whose present attitudes were represented by, *The Birth of a Nation* as a viral polity given to fits of enthusiasm in which fine phrases about reasons, causes, and ideals mask hidden logics of madness, with each successive action launched as a response to the excesses of the previous one in an endless cycle of self-correction and self-destruction—a return to a beginning point in an effort to get it right, only to get it tragically wrong once again. Neither Dixon nor Griffith invented this opinion. In his 1838 Lyceum speech, Abraham Lincoln alluded to the nation's recurrent tendency to populist anarchy, which he described as a "mobocratic spirit"[13] that Alexis de Tocqueville, in

11. *Testimony Taken by the Joint Select Committee to Inquire into the Condition of Affairs in the Late Insurrectionary States* (Washington, DC, 1871–72), thirteen volumes.

12. The claim for the "second Klan" as an essentially mainstream force in American politics and culture has been made by Linda Gordon in *The Second Coming of the Ku Klux Klan: The Ku Klux Klan of the 1920s and the American Political Tradition* (New York: Livewright, 2017).

13. Abraham Lincoln, "The Perpetuation of Our Political Institutions," speech delivered at the Young Men's Lyceum of Springfield, Illinois, January 27, 1838, http://www.abrahamlincolnonline.org/lincoln/speeches/lyceum.htm.

Democracy in America, characterized in more comprehensive terms as a general tropism toward tyranny implicit in popular rule.

In Dixon's novel as in the film, all this churning is said to have been initiated by the presence in America of black people imported as slaves from Africa. The film begins with an intertitle written by Griffith himself stating that, "The bringing of the African to America planted the first seed of disunion," implying that, before this moment, the European settlers—schismatic religious groups declared unwelcome in their home countries, along with outcasts and adventurers of various kinds, all struggling to gain a toehold in an alien land populated by Indians—were unified, or at least could have been unified given time if not for this bad seed, which grew to the point where a reckoning was inevitable. As the desolated heirs of thousands of years of savagery and predisposed to servitude, black people, Dixon believed, could never be assimilated into a democracy based on responsible self-governance. Dixon's descriptions of black physicality—typically rendered in list form, as in "a thick-lipped, flat-nosed, spindle-shanked negro, exuding his nauseating animal odour"—were intended to excite in his readers the sense of a natural revulsion excited by black people in those like himself, "the highest type of man evolved in time" (*Clansman,* 273, 290).

Given the commonly held view of the ineradicable genetic differences and social incompatibility of the races, many felt that the path to the "more perfect union" of the Constitution, and indeed the survival of the nation, depended not on finding a way forward to the full equality of all citizens but on the ability of the nation to discover the right form of white supremacy, a form that would contain or control, if not altogether eliminate, the threat posed by black people to the unity of the nation. Dixon placed himself in this tradition, depicting the emergence of the Klan as the first post-emancipation assertion of the "Aryan" genius for leadership—not mobocracy, but a capacity for social self-regulation and self-reliance in which the people rather than centralized authority take the lead.

Largely forgotten today when he is not reviled, Dixon was not a fringe figure. Raised in the stressed circumstances of the post-war South, he had made his way by becoming a man of the word: an actor, a lawyer, a minister identified with the Social Gospel Movement, and an immensely successful lecturer who, according to one estimate, preached and lectured to five million people in a four-year period on such subjects as political corruption, women's rights, Cuban independence, and the plight of immigrants, slum dwellers, and otherwise disadvantaged and distressed people.[14] In time, he also became one of the most prolific and successful playwrights in the country, the author of eighteen novels, a movie producer, a real estate entrepreneur, and a supporter of Theodore Roosevelt. It is difficult to see Dixon's career as a single arc because near the end of the nineteenth century he experienced a mysterious and decisive break. Perhaps troubled by the imperial acquisition, in the Pacific and the Caribbean, of populations who—like American blacks, he may have thought—seemed incapable of self-rule, and perhaps provoked as a Southerner by seeing one of the hundreds of stage versions of *Uncle Tom's Cabin* that were then touring the country, Dixon became almost overnight a virulent racist, one of the people, as Griffith's biographer Richard Schickel says, "who must

14. The estimate is given by Raymond A. Cook and cited in Anthony Slide, *American Racist: The Life and Films of Thomas Dixon* 9 (Lexington: University Press of Kentucky, 2004), 23. For an example of Dixon's moralizing mode, see Thomas A. Dixon Jr., *The Failure of Protestantism in New York and Its Causes* (New York: The Strauss & Rehn Publishing Company, 1896), which outlines Dixon's view on both the benefits of slavery and the necessity of abolishing slavery, and denounces the inability of the Church to fulfill the purpose of Christianity, which he describes as "the uplifting and ennobling of the masses" (37).

share the heaviest responsibility for the radical deepening and broadening of race hatred that occurred during the first decades of the twentieth century."[15] It was a surprising transformation in that black Americans, having lost most of what they had gained during Reconstruction, were in no position to threaten white supremacy. So late, so seemingly unmotivated, and so total was Dixon's conversion that Schickel suspects impure motives: "one cannot help but think Dixon's vision of a racial apocalypse was at least partially created out of his nearly insatiable need for self-dramatization" (77).

Shortly after his revelation, Dixon turned to novel-writing, launching what would become a Klan trilogy beginning with *The Leopard's Spots* in 1902, followed by *The Clansman* (1905) and *The Traitor* (1907). The books sold a million copies each, but then Dixon decided to write and even act in a stage version of *The Clansman,* that, while condemned by some even in the South as a "riot breeder . . . designed to excite rage and race hatred,"[16] attracted appreciative audiences in both North and South as a defiant Southern riposte to *Uncle Tom's Cabin.* His connections helped. When Griffith finished editing *Birth of a Nation,* Dixon persuaded his friend from graduate school Woodrow Wilson, whose account of Reconstruction in *A History of the American People* is quoted several times in intertitles in the film, to screen it in the White House, an occasion described by Henry Louis Gates as "a zenith in horror—the highest point of the lowest low" of white backlash against Reconstruction.[17] Dixon's reputation

15. Schickel, *D. W. Griffith*, 77.

16. From *Chattanooga Daily Times*, 1905; cited in Slide, *American Racist*, 60.

17. Henry Louis Gates, *Stony the Road: Reconstruction, White Supremacy, and the Rise of Jim Crow* (New York: Penguin Press, 2019), xv. Wilson was one of Dixon's and Griffith's primary historical sources. See Woodrow Wilson, *A History of the American People*, vol. 5, *Reunion and Nationalization* (New York: Harper and Brothers, 1901). Oddly, Gates cites as an early

today, insofar as he has one, is as a racist, a chauvinist, and an ideologue, but his biographer notes that at the peak of his fame he "might well have been considered by many as a liberal."[18] He was not a religious bigot, and by comparison with many Americans of his time, would have qualified as philosemitic. Interestingly, he attacked and was attacked by the "second era" of the Klan whose growth was in large part fueled by his work, describing them as "unprincipled marauders" and a "menace to American democracy" especially by comparison with the Klan of post-war period that he had portrayed as "an institution of Chivalry, Humanity, Mercy, and Patriotism" (*Clansman,* 320).[19] Near the end of his life, having lost nearly all his money through crashes and speculative failures, Dixon, by then a vehement anti-Communist ideologue, was appointed by Franklin Delano Roosevelt to a position as clerk to a federal court.

A fellow Southerner and son of a Confederate soldier and Klan member ("Roaring Jake" Griffith), Griffith was deeply familiar with views like Dixon's. He undoubtedly heard them voiced by Dixon himself when, in 1906, the very height of Dixon's fame, Griffith acted in one of Dixon's plays. The following year Griffith left acting for the new medium of film, working first as

---

influence on his thinking a course on the Harlem Renaissance he took as a Yale undergraduate in 1969–70 taught by Professor David Griffith, who is surely no relation to the filmmaker.

18. This is the judgment of Dixon's biographer Anthony Slide in *American Racist,* 18.

19. "Unprincipled Marauders," Dixon speech in 1923, cited in Kenneth J. Jackson, *The Ku Klux Klan in the City 1915–1930* (New York: Oxford University Press, 1967), 131. "Menace to democracy," quoted in "Dixon Condemns Klan," *New York Times*, August 5, 1924, 18; quoted in Slide, *American Racist*, 16. For the impact of *Birth of a Nation* on Klan recruitment efforts, see Stokes, *D. W. Griffith's* The Birth of a Nation, 231–41; and Jackson, *Ku Klux Klan*, 3–4. As a white supremacist, Dixon felt that it was the duty of the stronger and superior race "to lift up and help the weaker race" (Dixon, cited in Jackson, *Ku Klux Klan*, 176).

a writer and then as a director of one-reel melodramas and other entertainments at American Biograph in New York. Unhappy with the limitations the company imposed on him, and with the fact that they had fired him, Griffith was looking for a big project in 1913 when an associate, Frank Woods, suggested *The Clansman* as the basis for a film. In his autobiography, Griffith says he "skipped quickly through the book until I got to the part about the Klansmen. . . . I could just see these Klansmen in a movie with their white robes flying."[20] Griffith had apparently flipped through the first ninety percent of Dixon's talky, overwrought, and argumentative book, with its tangled and improbable plot—as a craftsman, Dixon is something of a lost cause—until he got to the part that appealed to him as a film-maker, the charge of the Klan (which in fact never happens in the novel; Klan horsemen ride, but do not gallop in pursuit). For Dixon, the book, the play, and the film were all directed toward the creation of a national consensus about white supremacy. The equally ambitious Griffith was more immediately interested in personal supremacy in his profession. As his mystified biographer—who had suspected Dixon of opportunism in his sudden conversion to virulent racism—says, Griffith's "motives appear to have been quite pure."[21]

It is difficult to gauge the level of agreement or even engagement that Griffith had with Dixon's ideas. Commentators have had recourse to notions of "unconscious" or "passive" racism, but the record is mixed and scanty; according to Schickel, "there is no evidence that any thought was devoted [by Griffith] to the racist implications of Dixon's story" (213). Griffith made approximately five hundred films on countless subjects—nine feature films in 1914–1915 alone, including *Birth of a Nation*—without

20. Griffith, "The Hollywood Gold Rush," 88.

21. Schickel, *D. W. Griffith,* 213. According to Schickel Griffith's spirit "was classically that of the artist—self-absorbed, and only dimly aware of the larger political issues of the day" (81).

considering them statements of his personal convictions, of which in any event he had very few. On most of the burning social issues of the day, including race, Griffith was conventional and unreflective; one might say that he "entertained" Dixon's views in that he converted them into entertainment without challenging them because he did not take them as seriously as Dixon. He was not a deep thinker or a man with a relentless social conscience. He favored peace but loved good stories, which generally involved conflict. Noting Griffith's "fundamental decency" and innocently romantic view of history, Schickel offers, rather half-heartedly, only "a plea of invincible political and social ignorance" (238). Like others, Agee regarded Griffith as a dreamer or a poet; indeed, Agee said, his respect for Griffith as an artist only increased when he considered Griffith's "handicaps," including "no remarkable power of intellect, or delicateness of soul; no subtlety; little restraint; little if any 'taste,'" an inability to understand people, a "pathetically crude" sense of humor, no capacity for change or growth, an exorbitant appetite for cruelty "and for the Siamese twin of cruelty, a kind of obsessive tenderness which at its worst was all but nauseating."[22] Griffith's understanding of the human condition was compatible with and perhaps informed by nineteenth-century melodrama, with its pathos, its mannerisms, its reassuring antipodes of good and evil.[23]

Indifferent to large, controversial, and intractable issues, and deeply committed to conventional genres and sentiments, Griffith saw the South in the terms he learned from the adults during his childhood, as an "eternal romance" involving battles,

22. James Agee, "David Wark Griffith," 315.

23. The case for the influence of melodrama on Griffith is made by Ben Singer in "Griffith's Moral Profile," in Charlie Keil, ed., *A Companion to D. W. Griffith* (Hoboken, NJ: John Wiley & Sons, 2018), 37–42. The first to raise the suggestion was Sergei Eisenstein, "Dickens, Griffith, and the Film Today," in Jay Leyda, ed. and trans., *Film Forum: Essays in Film Theory* (New York: Harcourt, Inc., 1949), 195–255.

bloodshed, and bravery.[24] He was often oblivious to the implications or offensiveness of his own statements. His praise of the "faithful souls" among the ex-slaves falls into this category, as does a 1916 comment about the decision "to have no black blood among the principals" on the set of the movie, and to use black actors only as "extra people."[25] When responses to the film, many which were at first ecstatic, began to include criticism and even condemnation, Griffith was bewildered, shocked, and disappointed by a public so obtuse it could not recognize a masterpiece when it saw one. As late as 1930, he said, in the course of a filmed conversation with Walter Huston about *Birth of a Nation,* with both men in evening dress in front of a roaring fire, that "the Klan at that time was needed . . . it served a purpose."[26] At that moment, Griffith had just finished one of his last films, and first talkie, a sentimental and admiring depiction of Abraham Lincoln.

If Griffith had not made *Birth of a Nation,* it would be difficult to describe his work as racist, for the film is an anomaly in a career occasionally distinguished by films characterized by a spirit of liberality and compassion. One of his most remarkable,

24. Griffith, quoted by Henry Stephen Gordon, "The Story of David Wark Griffith: Part Five," in Anthony Slide, ed., *D. W. Griffith: Interviews* (Jackson: University of Mississippi Press, 2012), 60. In the same interview, Griffith said that his first reading of *The Clansman* stirred "that regional impulse that comes to all men from the earth where they had their being stirred potently" (59).

25. Griffith, quoted in Gordon, 60.

26. The conversation between D. W. Griffith and Walter Huston was issued with an abbreviated sound version of *Birth of a Nation* in 1930; available in *Griffith Masterworks* (2002). The interview is online at https://www.youtube.com/watch?v=8PrYrRt-M1s. For a full account of the early reception of the film, see Arthur Lennig, "Myth and Fact: The Reception of *The Birth of a Nation,*" *Film History* 16 (April 2004) 2: 1–34. See also Stokes, *D. W. Griffith's* The Birth of a Nation, Chapters 5 and 6, 111–70; and Schickel, *D. W. Griffith,* Chapter 10, 267–303.

Broken Blossoms (1919), portrays the tragedy of interracial love in an intolerant society, and several others are sympathetic to Native Americans, including *The Redman's View* (1909), *The Indian Runner's Romance* (1909), *A Mohawk's Way* (1910), and *The Squaw's Love* (1911). Since Griffith also made other films in which Indians were depicted as violent savages, however, it seems that he had no strong personal views about Indians at all. Nor does he seem to have any personal animus against black people, typically describing his relations with them in paternalistic terms, as those of "affection and brotherly feeling."[27]

As Hannah Arendt argued in the case of Adolf Eichmann, obliviousness is no excuse, and thoughtlessness can be a particular, and particularly revealing form of thought.[28] In fact, the case against Griffith may be stronger than that against Dixon, who at least stated his views clearly and defended them stoutly. But Griffith's incomprehension of the issues raised by his own work complicates any attempt to see that work as the expression of his deeply held views or beliefs. Rather than treat the film as evidence of Griffith's perhaps nonexistent, sentimentalized, or blurry convictions, then, it would be more productive simply to assess how black people are presented in the film. This is not a question about Reconstruction, or Jim Crow America, or the private thoughts of Griffith or Dixon, although all these factors played some role. It is, rather, a question about representations, and about the inferences that viewers might draw from them if they did not feel constrained to see the film as an expression of the creator's intentions. To detach the film from its creators is to

27. D. W. Griffith, "The Birth of a Nation" from *Sight and Sound* 16, no. 61 (Spring 1947): 32. Agee actually makes the almost preposterous claim that Griffith "went to almost preposterous lengths to be fair to the Negroes as he understood them," adding that "he understood them as a good type of Southerner does" ("David Wark Griffith," 313).

28. Hannah Arendt, *Eichmann in Jerusalem: A Report on the Banality of Evil* (New York: Penguin, 1994).

make it possible to see it as something other than incontrovertible evidence of the wickedness of a few people or even of a disgraceful national past now safely quarantined from the present. The argument, then, is that *The Birth of a Nation* can be considered as documentary evidence of a necessarily incomplete and unfinished struggle to found a nation that reconciles ahistorical principles of equality with its actual conduct and actual history, a struggle that has characterized the nation from the beginning and that continues to the present day. Considered under this aspect, the film is not a representation of the struggle but is part of the struggle itself, and in that respect participates in the present whenever that present happens to be.

The subject of race is a good starting-point for this kind of analysis. The accusation is that the black people in *Birth of a Nation* are portrayed in unrealistic and insulting ways. One frequently mentioned example is the scene in the South Carolina Legislature, which Dixon describes as a "minstrel farce. . . . Beneath those loud guffaws [of the black legislators] they could hear the death-rattle in the throat of their beloved state, barbarism strangling civilization by brute force" (*Clansman,* 267). Many whites, especially in South Carolina, the only state in which blacks held a majority at any time during Reconstruction, were shocked by the spectacle of black people suddenly in positions of authority. An 1874 cartoon in *Harper's Weekly* called "Colored Rule in a Reconstructed (?) State" by Thomas Nast—at one time an ardent abolitionist—registers this shock, depicting a chaotic scene in a Reconstruction legislature, with black legislators shouting and threatening each other while the powerless whites in the chamber observe the spectacle in disgust.[29] But

29. The cartoon is reproduced in Eric Foner, *Reconstruction: America's Unfinished Revolution, 1863–77,* updated edition (New York: HarperPerennial, 2014), 386; see also Gates, *Stony the Road,* 153. Among the white people who observed the South Carolina Legislature in disgust were the young Thomas Dixon, Jr. and his uncle. See Raymond A. Cook, *Fire from the*

are the depictions in *The Clansman* and *Birth of a Nation* of black people in the government—the inevitable telos of Emancipation and thus the point of the Civil War—entirely reducible to a single-minded argument for black inferiority? Is there no other way of reading them that might yield a richer and more comprehensive understanding of the film, the culture documented in the film, and the culture in which the film was produced?

We should begin by considering the remarkable fact that of the two hundred and thirty-nine black men who served in the black majority in the South Carolina state legislature and state senate during the Reconstruction years, at least one hundred and thirty-one had been slaves.[30] Detailed information about these men is not easy to find, but any slave in South Carolina would have been prevented from acquiring any education or forming any ambition; he would have been discouraged from independent thought or judgment and strongly encouraged in a habit of deference. Most of the black people he knew would have been in the same condition, as would his parents and grandparents, whoever they may have been. Every aspect of the treatment of the slave was intended to produce durable effects in his thoughts

---

Flint: The Amazing Careers of Thomas Dixon (Winston-Salem, NC: John F. Blair, 1968), 12.

30. Eric Foner, "South Carolina's Elected Black Officials during Reconstruction," in James Lowell Underwood and W. Lewis Burke, Jr., eds., *At Freedom's Door: African American Founding Fathers and Lawyers in Reconstruction South Carolina* (Columbia: University of South Carolina Press, 2000), 170. "Not surprisingly," Foner writes elsewhere, "a considerable number of black officials" especially in the rural black belt "had not enjoyed the advantages of an education." Eric Foner, *Reconstruction*, 359. See *passim.*, Chapter 8, "Reconstruction: Political and Economic," 346–411. For a comprehensive directory, see Eric Foner, *Freedom's Lawmakers: A Directory of Black Officeholders during Reconstruction*, revised edition (Baton Rouge: Louisiana State University Press, 1996).

and behavior.[31] White people, especially slaveowners, understood the flattening, deadening effects of slavery, and many did everything in their power to produce and compound those effects. Moreover, as many observers including Du Bois noted, the situation for black people was actually worse in some ways after the war, when they lacked any protections from the whites with whom they were now competing. Du Bois described the shock and disorientation experienced by black men who had passed their lives in the "peculiarly complete system of slavery, centuries old," and who found themselves suddenly set free in a hostile world at the end of the Civil War.[32] It could surprise no one if individuals so conditioned did not, at the moment of emancipation, immediately conform to the mores of polite white society, which, for its part, had given them no reason or incentive to emulate any white models at all.

Deprived of positive models, black people would still have learned from whites how those in positions of power comported themselves. Much of the behavior by blacks that is condemned in the book and in the film—brutality, drunkenness, abusiveness, insolence, interracial lust, corruption—could be considered not

31. On this point see Alexis de Tocqueville, *Democracy in America and Two Essays on America*, trans. Gerald E. Bevan (New York: Penguin Books, 2003), especially Chapter 10, where he takes up the inferior position of black people, which he attributes not to their nature but to the oppression they suffer as slaves: "The Negro, plunged in this abyss of suffering, scarcely feels his ill fortune; violence had enslaved him, habituation to slavery has given him a slave's thoughts and ambitions . . . His intelligence has sunk to the level of his soul . . . Thus, he has reached such depths of wretchedness that slavery brutalizes him and freedom destroys him" (372).

32. W. E. B. Du Bois, "Of the Dawn of Freedom," *The Souls of Black Folk*, in *W. E. B. Du Bois Writings*, ed. Nathan Huggins (New York: Penguin Random House, 1986), 378.

as the actions or tendencies of black people suddenly free to act naturally, but as black mimicry of white behavior. In Nast's cartoon, the figure of Columbia tells the misbehaving black legislators, "You are aping the lowest Whites." To condemn Dixon's portrayal of black people as stereotypical or caricatural does not do justice either to the poverty of Dixon's imagination—his white characters are also caricatural, and both his book and Griffith's film could be considered slanders on the white race[33]—or to the effects of slavery, which could cripple a person long after his or her servitude had legally ended. Without crediting Griffith with any intention of this kind, then, it might then be possible to consider his work not only as a failed or malicious attempt at an accurate depiction of black people considered as human beings but also as a graphic representation, almost a confession, of the fully intended effects on human beings of chattel slavery.

And what about the actual performance of the black legislators shown in the film? The manifest intent of Dixon and Griffith is to show that black people were unworthy to be entrusted with political responsibility because they lacked the capacity to govern themselves, much less anyone else. Dixon and Griffith both claimed factual accuracy for their works, and Griffith was indignant at charges that he had falsified history, but the history on which both relied has itself been called into question. The prevailing authority on Reconstruction at the time was William A. Dunning, whose *Essays on the Civil War and Reconstruction* (1897) argued that Reconstruction had been a tragic mistake, a program of vengeance and hatred imposed on the South that had only been terminated through the efforts of brave and decent white Southerners. Noting that black suffrage was imposed on

33. The possibility that *The Clansman* was a slander on the white race was first suggested by Reverend Dr. L. G. Broughton of the Atlanta Baptist Tabernacle in 1905; cited in Slide, *American Racist*, 60. The ultimate source of the Broughton quote is the scrapbooks of Booker T. Washington housed at the Library of Congress.

the South by the federal government, which allowed Northern states to decide the matter for themselves, Dunning depicted Southern black legislators as ignorant barbarians doing the bidding of carpetbaggers, who sought only to ensure state governments loyal to the reconstituted Union. The "Dunning School" was largely unchallenged until 1935, when Du Bois published *Black Reconstruction in America,* in which, in a spectacular diatribe near the end of the book, he condemned Dunning and others for presenting under-researched white supremacist propaganda as history, and for ignoring a mass of archival evidence demonstrating that, on the whole, black people had performed reasonably well, and often admirably, during Reconstruction.[34]

34. Du Bois's condemnation of the Dunning School, while ignored by the scholarship of the day, has been confirmed and amplified by subsequent historians of Reconstruction, including John Hope Franklin, Eric Foner, Kenneth M. Stampp, and Leon F. Litwack. See especially Foner, *Reconstruction*, which points out that "the educated, articulate, and politically experienced freeborn delegates of South Carolina and Louisiana played major roles in their conventions, dominating debate and often outmaneuvering white participants" (319). Condemned by these later historians for arguing that enfranchising black people was a monstrous error, Dunning was among the first university-trained historians in the United States and developed other arguments about Reconstruction that remain pertinent and even unchallenged. Foner notes that his book, which sought to drive "the final nail in the coffin of the Dunning School," was supported by Yale's Dunning Fund (xxxi). For a recent reassessment, see John David Smith and J. Vincent Lowery, eds., *The Dunning School: Historians, Race, and the Meaning of Reconstruction* (Lexington: University Press of Kentucky, 2013). For an entirely different view of the matter, a deeply qualified defense of one of Dunning's arguments, see Adam Fairclough, "Was the Grant of Black Suffrage a Political Error? Reconsidering the Views of John W. Burgess, William A. Dunning, Eric Foner on Congressional Reconstruction" *Journal of the Historical Society* 12, no. 2 (June 2012): 155–88. Fairclough argues that Reconstruction was so badly designed and enforced that "it is hard to imagine that blacks, the South, and the nation would have been worse off under a program that stopped short of black suffrage" (187).

Du Bois would undoubtedly make the same accusation of bias against Dixon and Griffith; but interestingly, and again surely despite their intentions, Dixon and Griffith manage to present a picture of governance under Reconstruction that supports Du Bois's claim.[35]

Consider the scene in *Birth of a Nation* in which carpetbaggers urge black people, at a chaotic meeting of the Union League, to consider such measures as "Equal Rights," "Equal Politics," and "Equal Marriage." The list of such legislative absurdities given in *The Clansman* is more extensive:

> . . . a measure to disarm the whites and equip with modern rifles a Negro militia . . . to prevent any person calling another a "nigger" . . . to force whites and blacks to attend the same schools and open the State University to negroes; to permit the intermarriage of whites and blacks; and to enforce social equality (268).

Most American audiences in the twenty-first century would not find this list absurd. The first proposal is a mirror of white restrictions on black people owning firearms, a reversal that might have been considered by an impartial observer, if any could be found, to be unfair and undemocratic but perhaps necessary in order to prevent massacres, which in fact, subsequently occurred. The second represents a difficult issue of ongoing pertinence whose monitoring has been allocated to society at large, with mixed results. The third and fourth are today unchallenged laws

35. For an account of Du Bois's efforts, see David Levering Lewis, *W. E. B. Du Bois: Biography of a Race 1968–1919* (New York: Henry Holt and Company, 1993), 506–9. Du Bois, operating through the NAACP, failed to suppress the film, and may, as he admitted, have helped to publicize it. However the legal battle also drew national attention to the NAACP, so that, as Lewis notes, the film and the organization "helped make each other" (507).

Meeting of the Union League

of the land, and the fifth represents a goal to which a just nation must aspire.

By present lights, then, if not by Griffith's or Dixon's, this agenda is overall rational, fair, and humane. Indeed with respect to education and social equality, it envisions a more progressive program than any state in the union has been able to achieve to date. However even in the Reconstruction years, the black-majority South Carolina Legislature during this time of supposed barbarism, drunkenness, lewdness, and ignorance managed to pass, over vehement white opposition, a state constitution that created a statewide public school system, established universal suffrage, abolished many of the more medieval punishments, enlarged the rights of women, created a divorce law, outlawed dueling, and provided special education for the hearing- and speech-impaired. During these years South Carolina College (subsequently the University of South Carolina) was integrated and democratized, and Charleston's streetcars were successfully integrated—in both cases against white opposition. As Eric Foner says, most of the Southern conventions during this time "produced modern, democratic documents," often including language from the Declaration declaring all men equal; in a comment especially true of South Carolina, Foner writes that "politics and government were the most integrated institutions in Southern life" (*Reconstruction,* 319, 372). All this makes an inspiring story, and *Birth of a Nation* shows it—and, by presenting it as if it were contemptible, white resistance to it—happening.[36]

The episode in the film that has drawn the sharpest criticism is also the trigger for the action toward which the entire film builds, the spontaneous formation of the Klan. Inflamed by talk of marriage equality, Gus, a former slave of the Camerons ("the young scamp we used to own") pursues the teen-aged Flora Cameron up a cliff, scuttling and lurching after her, frothing at the mouth (*Clansman,* 191). In Dixon's novel, Gus actually rapes her, and she and her mother fling themselves off the cliff rather than endure the shame of it. In the play version Dixon wrote, which was at many points the more proximate source for Griffith's film, Gus is captured, and confesses that Flora leaped to escape him. For some reason, Griffith constructed a very different sequence. In the film, Gus, described in an intertitle as a "product of the vicious doctrines spread by the carpetbaggers"—a victim of social conditioning rather than an unreflective self-determining brute—approaches Flora, who is innocently gamboling around the woods, drawing water from the spring and winking at a squirrel. Tipping his cap, he tells her with unpracticed

36. In *Black Reconstruction in America,* Du Bois describes the Reconstruction Legislature in South Carolina as the momentary triumph of a "black proletariat" in which "poor men were ruling and taxing rich men" (344). See especially Chapter X, "The Black Proletariat in South Carolina," 313–53. For a different assessment of the South Carolina Legislature during Reconstruction, see Thomas Holt, *Black over White: Negro Political Leadership in South Carolina during Reconstruction* (Champaign: University of Illinois Press, 1977). Using statistical methods in analyzing voting records, Holt argues that black leaders during this time were "basically bourgeois in their origins and orientations and oftener than not failed to act in the interests of black peasants" (3). Of particular interest is Appendix A, "Sources for Biographical Data on Negro Legislators," 225–41.

Gus suggests marriage to Flora Cameron

urgency that now that he is a Captain in the army, he wants to marry—her.[37] She does not seem at first surprised or alarmed, but after a brief exchange, she pushes him aside. He grabs her arm apparently to assure her of his sincerity, but she slaps his face and flees through the woods, waving her arms wildly. In a scene so visually compelling that early audiences reportedly stormed the stage to save her—the same audiences who fell back in horror a few minutes later when the Clansmen charged toward a receding camera—she ascends a rocky slope, with Gus following and swearing that he will not hurt her. She pauses on the precipice, he extends his arms—and she leaps unsullied to her death. Her outraged brother Ben, the former Confederate soldier, summons the Klan to avenge her death, put an end to the minstrel farce of black governance, and restore the honor of his race. Gus is captured and hung.

Like Dixon's descriptions of the physical Negro, the entire sequence is constructed as a stimulus to what Dixon described as "a feeling of abhorrence in white people, especially white

37. For some reason Henry Louis Gates, having described this scene as "perennially painful-to-watch," says that Gus "attempts to rape Flora Cameron" (*Stony the Road,* 154).

Flora loses her mind

women, against colored men,"[38] in the specific form of a fear of sexual violence by black men and, behind that, a more general dread of racial mixing, which would lead to a mongrelized species and social collapse. Useful to the cause of white supremacy, the figure of the marauding black rapist was almost entirely a creation of that fear, as more literate or informed Southerners probably suspected.[39] The massive 1871 report (accompanied by twelve volumes of "testimony taken") by the Joint Select Committee of Congress "to Inquire into the Condition of Affairs in the Late Insurrectionary States," produced evidence of hundreds of Negroes killed, shot, whipped, mutilated, or burned out—all of which went unpunished—but, according to Du Bois, no case of a white woman seduced or raped by a Negro in South Carolina.[40] Interracial rape was almost entirely the work

38. Dixon, quoted in "Fighting a Vicious Film: Protest Against *The Birth of a Nation*," pamphlet (Boston: Boston Branch of the National Association for the Advancement of Colored People, 1915); reprinted in Geduld, *Focus on D. W. Griffith*, 94.

39. On the discourse surrounding the "natural" propensity of black men to rape white women, and on lynching as a logical and necessary response, see Gates, *Stony the Road*, 141–48.

40. W. E. B. Du Bois, *Black Reconstruction in America: An Essay Toward a History of Part Which Black Folk Played in the Attempt to Reconstruct*

of white men, and every mixed-race person in the South was very likely evidence of the willingness of white men to set aside, for a few moments at least, their professed terror of racial mongrelization and professed contempt for a strange-smelling race of savages and slaves.[41] The avoidance by Dixon and Griffith of this manifest fact supports the charge that their treatment of race reflects nothing more than white panic, and the desire to excite white panic at the prospect of racial equality.

But surely one highly effective way to fan the flames of white supremacy would be to depict a realistic rape of a white woman by a black man. This was well within Griffith's powers.[42]

Democracy in American, 1860–1880 (New York: Oxford University Press, 2007), 554. The report to which Du Bois refers is *Testimony Taken by the Joint Select Committee to Inquire into the Condition of Affairs in the Late Insurrectionary States*. I have been unable to confirm his citation from this work, but for a contemporary account that confirms Du Bois's conclusion, see the autobiography of former Union General Oliver Otis Howard. He reports that in the state of Kentucky between June and October 1867, there were twenty-five murders, thirty-five assaults with intent to kill, eighty-three cases of assault and battery, four of rape, and four of arson. "But not one murderer anywhere in the State had been punished, and the majority of other criminals had escaped every penalty of the law." O. O. Howard, *Autobiography of Oliver Otis Howard*, 2 vols. (New York: Baker & Taylor, 1908), II: 344.

41. Public knowledge that one had raped a black woman was not even an impediment to social and political advancement, as the career of James Henry Hammond demonstrates. Already known to have raped his four nieces, Hammond then raped two of his slaves: one the daughter of the other and possibly his own daughter as well. An outspoken advocate of slavery, Hammond became a U.S. Representative, Senator, and Governor of South Carolina. See Drew Gilpin Faust, *James Henry Hammond and the Old South* (Baton Rouge: Louisiana State University Press, 1982). On the sexual abuse of slaves see Peter Kolchin, *American Slavery, 1619–1877* (New York: Hill & Wang, 1993), 120ff.

42. As journalist Tamar Lane wrote as early as 1923, Griffith "cannot seem to get away from the situation of the attacking, raping or wronging of the

A number of his films allude to rape as an extreme form of distress for a damsel to be in, and *Birth of a Nation* in particular is credited with having invented many of the conventions of cinematic realism. But Griffith ultimately declined to transcribe *The Clansman*'s rapist to his film (or to hang Gus merely for a woman's response to his proposal; in the film, Gus shoots an already-wounded white man who has come looking for him). In fact, the scene of the proposal and its dénouement has the character of a fantastical interlude, an evocation not of the imminent collapse of civilization but of Red Riding Hood in the forest.

The unreality-effect is greatly compounded by one of the most striking features of *Birth of a Nation,* the use of blackface. Many black characters are played by white actors, including the "faithful souls" who remain loyal to the Camerons; Gus, played by Walter Long, made, in the recollection of one man on the set, "no effort to look like a real Negro. He put on the regular minstrel-man blackface makeup, so there could be no mistake about who and what he was."[43] In fact, none of the blackface actors made any effort, not even those who played "white spies" who had infiltrated a black mob. (The mob was composed of black actors, who were, in the fiction of the film, deceived by burnt cork.) To many critics, this crudity locks in the case for Griffith's racism. One has argued that blackface proves that the film is "more about how whiteness imagines blackness than it is

---

defenseless girl . . . he hardly ever attempts to make a screen story without it." Tamar Lane, *What's Wrong with the Movies* (Los Angeles: The Waverly Company, 1923), 63. Moreover according to Seymour Stern, shots of "screaming white women being whisked by Negro rapists into doorways in the back alleys of the town were omitted after the initial showings" of the film. Seymour Stern, "Griffith: I—*The Birth of a Nation*," *Film Culture* 36, Special Griffith Issue (Spring-Summer, 1965): 66; cited in Stokes, *D. W. Griffith's* The Birth of a Nation, 295.

43. Karl Brown, *Adventures with D. W. Griffith*, ed., Kevin Brownlow (London: Secker and Warburg, 1973), 62.

about blackness itself."[44] And no less a figure than the distinguished film critic Andrew Sarris wrote that the use of blackface suggests that, for Griffith, "blackness itself [is] a state of being so inferior that blacks themselves are incapable of interpreting and communicating its inescapable baseness."[45] In an influential discussion of the subject in *Blackface, White Noise: Jewish Immigrants in the Hollywood Melting Pot*,[46] Michael Rogin argues that in the early years of the twentieth century, blackface constituted a particular form of racial aggression as a way for Jewish actors to ease their assimilation into mainstream American society, setting aside their own problematic ethnicity and miming real or imagined black qualities such as sensuality, *joie de vivre,* and musicality, thereby ingratiating themselves with the dominant culture but effectively silencing black Americans whose far more problematic color-coded ethnicity remained unassimilable.

This analysis may explain Al Jolson, but does it explain Gus?

44. Daniel Bernardi, "Integrating Race into the Narrator System," in Jeffrey Geiger and R. L. Rutsky, eds., *Film Analysis: A Norton Reader*, 2nd edition (New York: W. W. Norton), 59.

45. Andrew Sarris, "BIRTH OF A NATION or White Power Back When," in Fred Silva, ed., *Focus on "The Birth of a Nation,"* 108.

46. Michael Rogin, *Blackface, White Noise*; see especially Chapter Three, "Nationalism, Blackface, and the Jewish Question" (45–72). Rogin is also the author of an important scholarly essays on Griffith, "'The Sword Became a Flashing Vision': D. W. Griffith's *The Birth of a Nation*," *Representations* 9 (Winter 1985): 150–95; reprinted in Robert Lang, ed., *The Birth of a Nation* (New Brunswick, NJ: Rutgers University Press, 1994), 250–93. Lang's book also contains a "continuity script" tracking every shot in the film, and Dixon's and Griffith's responses to an attack published in the *New York Globe*. On blackface, see also W. T. Lhamon, Jr., *Raising Cain: Blackface Performance from Jim Crow to Hip Hop* (Cambridge, MA: Harvard University Press, 1998); and Brian Roberts, *Blackface Nation: Race, Reform, and Identity in Popular Music, 1812–1925* (Chicago: University of Chicago Press, 2017).

Critics of Griffith's use of blackface often imply that a more humane, less morally compromised director would have staged a more nuanced and authentic representation of blackness. Combining the nineteenth-century minstrel show, in which even black performers used blackface, with the fairy tale, Gus's performance insists on its own artifice, which is to say its own falseness. But a more realistic representation of Gus's pursuit with, for starters, a black actor would only have confirmed white fears in a horrifying and explicit way, as well as being unrealistic in the sense of being demonstrably untrue to historical experience. Having a white man who is obviously painted black pretend in cartoonish fashion to propose an act of miscegenation that, in the world, was almost always committed by white men, almost always outside wedlock, and very often without any ritual of courtship or formal proposal, draws attention to this untruth, and points directly to a deeper reality. With what level of intentionality or awareness one can only surmise, Griffith manages to lay bare, in well-nigh Brechtian fashion, a compost of white racial fear, desire, and guilt, presenting it in a manner that all but states outright that white people imagine black people to have desires they themselves have, punish them for crimes they themselves commit, and blame them for the racial mixing they themselves both produce and deplore.[47] In short, the most emotionally powerful

47. This aspect of Griffith's film seems almost designed to illustrate the principle of reversal described by Frederick Douglass in an 1863 speech: "Whenever and wherever men have been oppressed and enslaved, their oppressors and enslavers have in every instance found a warrant for such oppression and enslavement in the alleged character of their victims. The very vices and crimes which slavery generates are usually charged as the peculiar characteristic of the race enslaved." Douglass, "The Present and Future of the Colored Race in America," in Philip Foner, ed., *The Life and Writings of Frederick Douglass*, vol. III, *The Civil War 1861–65* (New York: International Publishers, 1952), 355. For a fascinating discussion of interracial sex in the eighteenth century, see Winthrop Jordan, *The White Man's Burden* (London: Oxford University Press, 1974), Chapter 4, "Fruits of

Elsie Stoneman loses her mind at the thought of marriage to Lynch

and direct exposé of the fantasies that lie at the heart of American racism can be found not in the criticisms of Griffith's film but in the film itself.

The fear of mongrelization and the unreality of blackface converge again in the two mixed-race, or "mulatto" figures in the film. The first, Senator Stoneman's treacherous protégé Simon Lynch, gets himself elected Lieutenant Governor of South Carolina, and then declares to his horrified benefactor his intention to marry Stoneman's daughter Elsie (Lillian Gish) and —somehow setting aside the fact that any issue of their union would be three-quarters white—make her the queen of a "Black Empire." Stunned, the Great Commoner and architect of Reconstruction slumps into a chair from which he is unable to rise as Lynch unfolds his plans to Elsie, who, like Flora, loses her mind and runs frantically around the room, finally fainting and

Passion: The Dynamics of Interracial Sex, 69–86. "It is apparent," Jordan writes, "that white men projected their own desires onto Negroes" (80). Jordan also notes that during this time liaisons between white women and black men were more common in the South Carolina back country than elsewhere (77).

Lydia Brown contemplates racial equality

remaining unconscious for many minutes. Eventually she is saved, and Lynch captured, by the Klan.

The other, even more consequential, mulatto is Stoneman's wild-eyed housekeeper Lydia Brown, modeled on Lydia Hamilton Smith, who lived with Thaddeus Stevens and ran his household. Brown fancies herself the first lady of the land, and performs elaborate rituals of condescension and insolence even to distinguished guests. Following Dixon, Griffith suggests that Reconstruction was largely her doing. This "strange brown woman," as Dixon describes her, "a mulatto, a woman of extraordinary animal beauty and the fiery temper of a leopardess," had somehow seduced and bewitched Stoneman, pouring wild dreams of racial equality into his ear (*Clansman,* 57). "No more curious or sinister figure ever cast a shadow across the history of a great nation than did this mulatto woman in the most corrupt hour of American life," Dixon writes (about a woman who, after Stevens's death invested in real estate and became the owner of a boarding house in Washington). Stoneman, Dixon writes, was under her power and the nation was under his: "the grim old man who looked into her sleek tawny face and followed her catlike eyes was steadily gripping the Nation by the throat" (94). In Dixon's account, the most powerful and personally ferocious politician in the country is unable to keep his wits about him in the presence of a mulatto woman. At the end of *The Clansman,* a repentant Stoneman realizes the great damage his policies have wrought, and in a moment of revelation blames it all on her: "When I first fell a victim to the wiles of the yellow vampire who kept my house, I dreamed of lifting her to my level. And when I felt myself sinking into the black abyss of animalism, I whose soul had learned the pathway of the stars and held high converse with the great spirits of the ages— . . . My life has been a failure" (371–72). Needless to say, this episode has no analogue in the life of Thaddeus Stevens, and the portrait of Lydia Brown no original in Lydia Hamilton Smith.

Dixon's mulattos are nightmare figures set loose in the human world to wreak havoc by scrambling the natural order of things —in the case of Simon Lynch by raising black people to a position of supremacy, and in the case of Lydia Brown by bringing white people down to a common animality. In both cases, mulattos are depicted not as instances of racial mixing or proof that the barrier between the races is easily and commonly breached, but as secret agents of black power who have managed to infiltrate and corrupt white society. They represent the deepest kind of threat to a "familial" principle of affiliation in which different but essentially compatible strains—the Camerons and the Stonemans, united in marriage at the end of the film—are merged into a newly composite American national identity, a family of families.[48] Griffith's mulattos play the horrifying roles Dixon

48. According to Walter Benn Michaels, a "nativist" or "familial" understanding of American national identity began in the 1920s to occupy a central position in American culture. At this time, Michaels argues, the concept of culture began to assume an all-but-racial character, supported by discourses that emphasized "blood" and "breeding" as the key to national identity. In the nativist model, various white people could consider themselves joined together without compromising the purity of American culture. The concept was implicitly or even explicitly racial in that certain groups—preeminently black people but also Jews and other nonwhite

assigned them, but with their thespian artifice so nakedly declared, they also demonstrate something else entirely, a reversibility based on a fundamental equivalence between races that runs contrary to the doctrine of white supremacy, but is central to the effects Griffith actually creates and to arguments that Dixon, undoubtedly without intending to, actually makes.

Perhaps unsurprisingly in a man who went from being a preacher for social justice to the nation's leading racist, reversibility is a kind of tic with Dixon, a default mode reproduced at many levels, beginning with conversations structured as duels between well matched adversaries, neither with an advantage. "The real issue," one man says, "is Democracy," to which the other replies, "The issue, sir, is Civilisation!" (291). Or, in a slightly more extended exchange:

"You are a conspirator—"

"I am a revolutionist."

"You are committing murder!"

"I am waging war." (335)

Such conversational standoffs are replicated at the level of plot, where the South Carolina Camerons mirror the northern Stonemans, each with children lost in the war, and each left with a son and a daughter, who end up in each other's arms. A tendency to the binary might be expected in a work that deals with the Civil War and the racial divide, or, for that matter, in a works such as *The Clansman* and *Birth of a Nation* that are so

---

people—were thought to represent unassimilable "foreign" elements. See Michaels, *Our America: Nativism, Modernism, and Pluralism* (Durham: Duke University Press, 1995). The concept of the clan could, in this understanding, become a model for the American family of families. In *The Clansman* Dixon writes of "American nationality" as being comprised of "Scotch folk from the North of Ireland," New England Puritans, "the so-called Cavaliers of Virginia," and French Huguenots. All these groups spread across the land, blending their forces while remaining "loyal to their own people, instinctive clan leaders and clan followers" (187–88).

manifestly indebted to melodrama, with its obligatory oppositions of vice and virtue, good and evil, male and female. But what Dixon and perforce Griffith add to this generic tendency is the sense that, appearances notwithstanding, the oppositions are unstable: the terms can trade places and the moral evaluations attaching to each term can be reversed.

At the core of Dixon's outrage over Reconstruction is the appalling symmetry of the fact that white people are now being made slaves by their former slaves, with, to use Woodrow Wilson's words, quoted on an intertitle, "the white South under the heel of the black South." As an indignant Dr. Cameron tells Stoneman, "No people in the history of the world have ever before been so basely betrayed, so wantonly humiliated and degraded!" (*Clansman*, 290). It does not occur to Dr. Cameron that his former slaves could say the same thing with greater justice. But what shocks Dr. Cameron does not shock Dixon, who compulsively constructs situations in which opposing terms, on scales ranging from great historical convulsions down to domestic exchanges, can suddenly become inverted, revealing a deeper identity.

This discovery lies at the heart of Dixon's, and to a lesser degree Griffith's, contribution to the theory of the nation, a contribution that cannot be grasped so long as the novel and the film based on it are seen as being wholly and solely expressions of a vicious racism. To get at this contribution, we have to look back through the film to the arguments made in the long first section of Dixon's novel, arguments that are registered but unstressed and easily overlooked in the film.

Many readers today would find those arguments surprising. The South is made to bear all the blame for slavery, Ben Cameron tells his future bride, but in fact, "the South is no more to blame for Negro slavery than the North . . . Our slaves were stolen from Africa by Yankee skippers. When a slaver arrived at Boston, your pious Puritan clergyman offered public prayer of thanks that 'A gracious and overruling Providence had been pleased to bring to this land of freedom another cargo of benighted heathen to enjoy the blessings of a gospel dispensation—'" (*Clansman,* 124). He goes on—and on—to point out that while abolitionist sentiment and calls for freedom were heard in Virginia and Carolina, the slave trade flourished in Massachusetts. His mother notes that Lincoln is revered in the South as the noblest soul and greatest man in the nation and is regarded with fondness and respect as a "Southern" president even as he is ridiculed and reviled in the North. On several occasions, Dixon's characters argue that Northerners are far more Negro-phobic than Southerners; Dixon even has Stoneman himself declare that, "The Negro will never be treated as an equal in the North. . . . To the Yankee the very physical touch of a Negro is pollution" (182). Near the end of the novel, Dr. Cameron tells Stoneman that "Every man in South Carolina to-day is glad that slavery is dead" (290).

Griffith registers most of these sentiments early on, but the great length of the film and the high drama of the conclusion have the effect of making them seem mere preliminaries if they are remembered at all. Reeling from the excitement of the triumphant charge of the Klan, viewers may be unable to recall the very beginning of the film, in which a Northern Abolitionist woman recoils in disgust at the smell of a slave boy. But this and other moments, in which the North is accused of crimes for which the South has borne the entire blame and the South claims virtues to which the North thought it had sole ownership, are crucial to the meta-argument of both novel and film.

Dixon became one of the most successful lecturers, novelists, and playwrights in the nation not because of his literary or oratorical brilliance alone but because he had a message the nation was eager to hear. Through his public speaking, his trilogy of Klan novels, his plays, and his collaboration with D. W. Griffith, Dixon played a critical role in the cultural movement known as the Lost Cause. This movement, now held in generally low regard as the desperate effort of a defeated force to reclaim some self-respect by indulging in delusions about the past, played a leading role in helping the nation bind up its wounds and re-establish the Union after the war.

Following Lee's surrender and the institution of Reconstruction, the great danger was that remnants of Confederate forces, seeing their states reduced to the status of internal colonies, would rise up in guerrilla revolt against both the federal government and the scalawags, carpetbaggers, and freedmen who now held the reins of power. It was in the interest of both North and South, if not of black people, to find a way for the white South to think well of itself and of the cause for which the war was fought. The war of ideas began directly after Appomattox, when elements of the Lost Cause, including the phrase, began to appear in post-war journalism and memoirs, and then in Southern literature.[49] Confederate veterans' organizations and

49. See especially Edward A. Pollard, *The Lost Cause: A New Southern History of the War of the Confederates* (War College Series: 2015); and *The Lost Cause Regained* (Scholarly Publishing Office, University of Michigan Library, 2005). On the contribution to Lost Cause ideology of other writers, especially those associated with The Southern Historical Society, see Richard D. Starnes, "Forever Faithful: The Southern Historical Society and Confederate Historical Memory," *Southern Cultures* 2 (Winter 1996) 2: 177–94. On the role played by Washington College (now Washington and Lee University), and specifically of Kappa Alpha fraternity, of which Dixon was a member, under the presidency of Robert E. Lee in the founding and early formation of the Klan, see Taulby Edmondson, "The Campus Confederate Legacy We're Not Talking About," *The Chronicle Review*, July 8, 2020: https://www.chronicle.com/article/The-Campus-Confederate-Legacy/249144?utm_source=at&utm_medium=en&utm_source=Iterable&utm_medium=email&utm_campaign=campaign_1346583&cid=at&source=ams&sourceId=1639206. On the backlash to Reconstruction, see Henry Louis Gates, *Stony the Road*, Part One, 1–54. On the religious element in the Lost Cause, see Charles Reagan Wilson, *Baptized in Blood: The Religion of the Lost Cause, 1865–1920* (Athens: University of Georgia Press, 2009).

magazines published beginning in the 1870s played a role in disseminating the Lost Cause throughout the South, but it was not until Dixon took it up that the movement coalesced into a compelling narrative about the war and its causes that could be accepted by the entire nation. As Henry Louis Gates writes,

> it can be argued that Dixon's interpretation of Reconstruction did more over the next several decades of the twentieth century to shape the country's understanding of that historical period, especially the supposedly noble origins of the Ku Klux Klan, than any other single factor . . . What *Uncle Tom's Cabin* had been to the abolition movement, *The Clansman* was to the Lost Cause and to Jim Crow white supremacist ideology (*Stony the Road*, 104–05).

In this narrative, the antebellum South was a place where older values of dignity, gentility, humaneness, valor, and chivalry prevailed in contrast to the hectic, moralizing, intolerant, profiteering culture of the North. While the North was becoming increasingly devoted to the hard, narrow virtues associated with expansion, wealth accumulation, and industrialization, the South stood for a traditional way of life, and especially for a commitment to forms of freedom and self-determination from which the North was turning away. It was this commitment, not slavery —and certainly not slavery as it was misunderstood by radical Abolitionists—that was the cause of the war; the problems associated with the presence of so many black people in the South were irritating distractions from the main issue. Secession was not an act of rebellion against the country as such but a protest against the internal tyranny increasingly practiced by the North and, rightly considered, a deeper form of patriotism. While the Confederate forces may have been defeated on the battlefield by the populous and wealthy Union, the true victory, in moral and cultural terms, went to the Confederacy. The program of

Reconstruction engineered by Thaddeus Stevens and the Radical Republicans was an insult to the pride of the South, a deeply misguided and hypocritical effort to create an impossible racial equality at a stroke, an equality that would never have been tolerated in the North. The Klan was a necessary response—disciplined, effective, principled, apolitical, peaceable, and, properly understood, patriotic—to the licensed horrors of Reconstruction, which one historian deeply sympathetic to the Klan writing in 1924 argued were worse than "the Massacre of St. Bartholomew" and "the thumb-screws or engines of torture of the Spanish Inquisition."[50] As the medieval crusaders had rescued the Holy Land from infidels, so the Klan reclaimed the South from its unworthy conquerors. Something of the self-heroizing spirit of the Lost Cause is captured by Ben Cameron at the very end of *The Clansman,* when he gazes in his mind's eye at a celestial Fiery Cross and announces to his beloved, "I am a successful revolutionist—Civilisation has been saved, and the South redeemed from shame" (*Clansman,* 374).

50. Susan Lawrence Davis, *Authentic History of the Ku Klux Klan, 1865–1877* (New York: Susan Lawrence Davis, 1924), 308. Davis, who grew up near the Pulaski, Tennessee, birthplace of the Klan, bases her history largely on statements she obtained from former Klan members, as well as on public documents, including two documents named "General Order #1," the first issued by the Tennessee Klan in 1867 and the second issued by Nathan Bedford Forrest, a former Confederate general then serving as the "Grand Wizard of the Invisible Empire," in 1869. Both speak of the Klan as an instrument for preserving public order and complain about the perversion of the Klan's original purposes by what Forrest calls "a few disobedient and bad men" who, taking advantage of the Klan's use of masks, had infiltrated the Order. They also engaged in unprincipled acts of violence anathema to the true Klan. As the Tennessee statement says, "These imposters have, in some instances, whipped negroes. This is wrong! Wrong!" "General Order #1," quoted in Davis, 107. Forrest, "General Order #1," quoted in Davis, 126.

The North—which, having prevailed, had no need to celebrate a Won Cause—was prepared to concede all this as the price of reunification. Through public celebrations and rituals of remembrance in which Confederate forces were treated as equal to the Union forces in terms of bravery, loyalty, and valor, the nation undertook the long process of healing, with the war itself now understood as a common ordeal, the focus of national remembrance rather than mutual slaughter with one victor. The ideology of the Lost Cause was thus an important factor in the reunification of the country, offering white Southerners not only a relief from any guilt they might have experienced over slavery, secession, and the slaughter of the war, but also a source of pride and a way of being American that was different from but morally equal to and in certain respects superior to that claimed by Northerners.[51]

Griffith's film told the story of the war from a Lost-Cause perspective in which North and South fought with equal valor and equal sacrifice for equally honorable causes, and told it to far more Americans than had ever before heard it, or indeed any story. In the second decade of the twentieth century, with major Civil War anniversaries being held, narrative films about the Civil War—eleven of them by Griffith—were nearly as popular as Westerns, which also played a role in sectional reintegration, but none was nearly so consequential as *Birth of a Nation.* One could say, then, that posterity owes an immense debt to Dixon and Griffith: they gave us the nation. It is, to be sure, a violent, delusional, schismatic, white-supremacist nation that they birthed, but it is one nation.

The matter does not rest there, however, because their film also contains energies that could be deployed in the service

51. See David W. Blight, *Race and Reunion: The Civil War in American Memory* (Cambridge, MA: Harvard University Press, 2001), 266ff.

of causes that are not lost, different voices that are not totally suppressed, and—the critical point—different nations within the federal nation.

Among the objections, condemnations, and calls for suppression that have for many years dominated the mainstream of *Birth of a Nation* criticism, there have always been those who felt that the film demanded some other kind of response. In 1918, the NAACP, frustrated by its inability to get the film banned, sponsored an abortive production called *The Birth of a Race* by John W. Noble that was intended as a response to Griffith. The film was artistically and financially unsuccessful, as was another made the following year by Oscar Micheaux, *Within Our Gates,* believed to be the oldest known surviving film by an African American director and also considered a response to Griffith. Quentin Tarantino's *Django Unchained* (2012) has been linked to *Birth of a Nation,* but the most significant responses to Griffith in recent years have been produced by three African American filmmakers, each of whom found Griffith's work worth recalling and even re-presenting.

Why? Why did Spike Lee devote his first film project as a student at New York University to a response to Griffith called "The Answer," about a black director chosen to do a remake of *Birth of a Nation*? And why, if Griffith's film is so singularly corrupting, did Lee include footage from it in his 2018 *BlacKkKlansman*? And how to explain the 2005 project undertaken by the sample artist Paul Dennis Miller, known as DJ Spooky, who, inspired by a 1956 essay by Guy Debord that recommended a possible "*détournement*" of the film—appropriating it but also "turning away" from it—produced a "remix" called *Rebirth of a Nation*? In this project, Miller compresses Griffith's film into half its original length, adds some graphics, tinkers with images so that at certain points a character is looking at a mirror image of himself, and, most significantly, adds a new soundtrack that replaces the heavily Germanic score that Griffith had commissioned by a heterodox assemblage of aural effects including what has been described as "a wash of industrial sounds."[52] And why did Nate Parker title his 2016 film about the 1831 slave revolt led by Nat Turner *The Birth of a Nation*? How have these artists managed to avoid the obligation to deplore and the impulse to suppress that have dominated criticism for many years, and what have they replaced them with?

We should begin by noting a tradition of African American responsiveness to the film. Richard Schickel alludes to documented statements from NAACP members who saw the film in 1915, and were, in their words, "swept up and away by it along with everyone else in the audience."[53] In a comprehensive study of the production, contexts, and consequences of *Birth of a Nation,* Melvyn Stokes records nearly a century of minority-report reviews by African American viewers who responded positively to the film.[54] Some, according to Stokes, admired the film's dramatic power, even to the point of cheering the Klan riders.[55]

52. Margo Jefferson, "Critic's Notebook; The Avant-Garde, Rarely Love at First Sight," *New York Times*, 8 July 2005, https://www.nytimes.com/2005/07/08/arts/movies/critics-notebook-the-avantgarde-rarely-love-at-first-sight.html. "Rebirth of a Nation" is also the name of a 2006 studio album by the hip-hop group Public Enemy and the rapper Paris. The title is the name of one of the singles on the album. For *détournement* see Guy-Ernest Debord and Gil J. Wolman, "Mode d'emploi du détournement" [Methods of Détournement], *Les Lèvres Nues* 8 (1956). The relevant passage on *Birth of a Nation* reads: "it is a racist film and therefore absolutely does not merit being shown in its present form . . . It would be better to detourn it as a whole . . . by adding a soundtrack that made a powerful denunciation of the horrors of imperialist war and of the activities of the Ku Klux Klan" Trans. Ken Knabb, https://www.cddc.vt.edu/sionline/presitu/usersguide.html.

53. Schickel, *D. W. Griffith*, 247.

54. Stokes, *D. W. Griffith's* The Birth of a Nation, 224–25.

55. In the late 1970s, the African American historian John Hope Franklin recorded the experience of hearing "nervous laughter and scattered

Others were charmed by the portrayal of the affection of former slaves for their masters. Still others felt that white actors in blackface could not be taken seriously, or that an ancient film was irrelevant to present concerns. Some responded positively to the depiction of a time when black people could not only vote but elect some of their own to positions of responsibility. And for some the sight of black people rising up in armed opposition to white people was invigorating and the murderous white response realistic.

Stokes does not mention another possibility that may come closer than any of these to explaining why a black artist or filmmaker in particular might choose to keep the film in the public conversation. The key to this possibility is the film's vivid reminder that nations are birthed in historical time. To see the nation not as a mystical or eternal entity but as the consequence of historical actions is to consider the possibility that the nation might be re-made, or perhaps remixed; it is to realize that the bonds linking the nation and the current distribution of power can be broken, with new possibilities arising. To think of the birth of a nation is to contemplate the possibility of a rebirth, which is to say, the birth of a different nation.

The United States of America could be said to have been born in 1776, or perhaps in 1789 with the adoption of the Constitution, or perhaps in 1865, when, following the Civil War, the nation began the process Lincoln had described at Gettysburg as "a new birth of freedom," sometimes referred to as a "second founding."[56] By titling his film *The Birth of a Nation*, Griffith

---

applause as the Klan begins its night ride." John Hope Franklin, "*Birth of a Nation*—Propaganda as History," *Massachusetts Historical Review* 20 (Autumn 1979) 3: 433.

56. The phrase, first uttered by Republican Congressman Carl Schurz before the Civil War, has been adopted by recent historians to describe the "Constitutional Revolution" effected by the thirteenth, fourteenth, and fifteenth amendments. These enshrined in the Constitution principles of

seems to reject all these birth dates and to propose another natal day in 1871, when Reconstruction had enabled blacks to form a majority in the South Carolina Legislature, provoking the events depicted in the film. Neither Dixon nor Griffith ever said exactly what nation was born in 1871 but two possibilities come to mind. The first, suggested by the film's final evocation of a unified polis, is a reborn United States of America, with the South integrated into a single nation. A recent history of the Klan makes just this case, arguing that despite its reactionary rhetoric and violence, the early Klan was dominated ideologically by the border and Northern states, and should be understood as an attempt by Southerners to adopt a post-war identity that would enable them to rejoin the Union. In this view, the emergence of the Klan was "part of a modernizing process . . . [that] permitted rural white southerners to move out of the Confederacy and into a new and integrated nation." While in an obvious sense the Klan represented an assertion of Southern interests against Northern claims to authority, at a deeper level, this historian argues, the Klan "served the purpose of sectional reconciliation and the construction of a shared set of political understandings between northerners and southern Democratic whites."[57] So ludicrously medieval and backward-looking in some respects, the Klan, in this view, actually represented a way for the South to abandon its ruined past and become integrated into a modern nation.

---

universal (male) citizenship and equal protection under the laws, to be enforced at the national level. See Eric Foner, *The Second Founding: How the Civil War and Reconstruction Remade the Constitution* (New York: W. W. Norton & Co., 2019).

57. Elaine Frantz Parsons, *Ku-Klux: The Birth of the Klan during Reconstruction* (Chapel Hill: University of North Carolina Press, 2015), 12. See also Allen Trelease, *White Terror: The Ku Klux Klan Conspiracy and Southern Reconstruction* (New York: Harper and Row, 1971), which focuses on the organizational structures of the early Klan.

But there is another way of thinking about the nation that arose in 1871, as a more complex and discordant entity in which the South, forced to concede the political and military power of the Union, asserted a far greater autonomy than it would have had if Reconstruction had proceeded unresisted. In this version of the nation, the post-war South clung to the tattered remnants of its traditions and constituted itself in thought if not in fact as a separate nation, a culturally and historically specific entity defined by geography, a history of shared sacrifice, and a determination to preserve itself against resistance from modernity and the federal state. This bootstrapping "Southern nation," as one recent book calls it, conceived of itself as a "nation within a nation," an unincorporated, self-defining and semi-autonomous entity, a collectively held idea rather than a set of instituted governmental or legal structures.[58] That book was published in 2018, but the concept of a nation within the nation was current in the antebellum South. In 1847, John C. Calhoun declared on the floor of the Senate that the country was never intended by its founders to be a single nation, but rather a Union, a "constellation of nations," adding that this was "a far more brilliant and striking conception" than the federalism into which the nation had fallen.[59]

These seem to be two utterly different concepts—the powerful modern nation including the forgiven but proud and forward-looking South, and the fragile and factional Union including the beaten but unrepentant and regressive South, which thought of itself as a semi-independent nation. But neither concept was entirely accurate. The authors of *Southern Nation* make the point

58. David A. Bateman, Ira Katznelson, and John S. Lapinski, *Southern Nation: Congress and White Supremacy after Reconstruction* (Princeton, NJ: Princeton University Press, 2018), 3.
59. John C. Calhoun, "Remarks Made in the Senate," 20 February 1847, in Richard K. Crallé, ed., *The Works of John C. Calhoun*, vol. 4 (New York: D. Appleton & Co., 1854), 355.

that, over the course of the century following the Civil War, Southern politicians were able to exercise such influence over national policy on race that they were able to make "the whole of the United States into a Southern nation," an outcome Calhoun could scarcely have dreamed of (3). As the century turned, the nation kept finding new reasons and ways to accommodate the sensitivities of the South, beginning by granting the South a kind of home rule with respect to race. When Reconstruction ended, Southern states were free to devise ways to exclude or limit black people from voting, as many Northern states, including Connecticut and Massachusetts, had done from the first.[60] American military bases throughout the South were named after heroes of the Confederacy, now recast as American patriots.[61] The Jim Crow laws mandating resegregation and discrimination that began to appear in the South in 1890 spread unchecked into the North, where segregation was practiced to a degree unimaginable in the South. Ultimately, thirty-six states adapted Jim Crow laws, encountering no resistance from the Supreme Court, one of whose chief justices, Edward D. White (1910–21), a former Louisiana Klansman, had seen *Birth of a Nation* the day after Wilson had screened it at the White House. Half a century after the end of the war, the nation seemed to have taken as a principle of social progress the reversibility first given form in *The Clansman* and then dramatized and disseminated in *The Birth of a Nation.*

Griffith intuitively understood the potential of film, and his film in particular, to shape public consciousness, saying that he

60. After the Civil War, proposals for black suffrage went down to defeat in Minnesota, Ohio, and Kansas. Other states had various restrictions that effectively excluded them. See Eric Foner, *Reconstruction*, 315.

61. See Editorial Board, *New York Times*, "Why Does the U. S. Military Celebrate White Supremacy?" May 23, 2020, https://www.nytimes.com/2020/05/23/opinion/sunday/army-base-names-confederacy-racism.html?action=click&module=Opinion&pgtype=Homepage.

named the film *The Birth of a Nation* "because it is . . . The Civil War was fought fifty years ago. But the real nation has only existed in the last fifteen or twenty years . . . The birth of a nation began, according to an authority [then-President Woodrow Wilson], with the Ku Klux Klans, and we have shown that."[62] This strangely off-center comment, floating an uncertain referent for "it," manages to insinuate two more possible birth dates for the nation, which is to say two more possible nations: the turn of the century, when the Lost Cause was gaining traction, and 1915, when his film gave masses of people a national story they could all, or at least large numbers of them, salute.

What is a nation? When he posed this question in 1882, Ernest Renan knew nothing about the viral power of film, but his answer to this question can help us understand why African American artists found Griffith's work so useful, so good to think, so worth preserving and reanimating. Renan begins by noting that nations are recent arrivals on the world geopolitical scene, that they are invented rather than given, and that they represent principles of freedom and self-determination in opposition to theological, imperial, or overly centralized power. A nation, Renan says, is based not on language, race, religion, geography, or dynastic succession alone, but above all on a common identity, a "soul" or "spiritual principle" to which all assent.[63] An act of unification is necessary in order to clarify and assert this common identity because all nations are composites of people who have consented to the union and agreed to live together as if they were one. This composite is both the strength and the weakness of the nation. Because the national fusion is "always

62. "D. W. Griffith, Producer of the World's Biggest Picture," interview with D. W. Griffith, *New York American*, February 28, 1915; in Geduld, *Focus on D. W. Griffith*, 28. The "authority" in question may well be Woodrow Wilson.

63. Ernest Renan, "What is a Nation?" I have used the translation by Ethan Rundell, http://ucparis.fr/files/9313/6549/9943/What_is_a_Nation.pdf.

brutally established," the viability of the nation depends on a determined "forgetting" of the means by which the end of the nation was achieved—a forgetting, that is, of the birth of the nation. The "daily plebiscite" that is the nation is always threatened by the eruption of bad memories. Historians can be enemies of the state; as Renan warns, "the progress of historical studies often poses a threat to nationality." And so, he concludes, "forgetting, I would even say historical error, is an essential factor in the creation of a nation . . . For everyone, it is better to forget."

Everyone, that is, except for those who want to destabilize the nation by questioning its origins, thereby troubling the national narrative and laying the groundwork for a new or reborn nation founded on a different narrative. This is one way of thinking of the project of Griffith's film, whose title represents a claim that the post-war rise of the Klan (a "veritable Empire of the South," as Wilson put it) represents the full flower of the seed planted by the Revolution, the true birth of the nation.

Griffith rests this claim largely on Wilson's scholarship, but scholarship is an unreliable ally, for its premise is that all conclusions are provisional and can in principle be improved, modified, or disproven. All nations are vulnerable to new research that reveals that the narrative that serves as the ground of national identity is not just an "imagined community," in Benedict Anderson's famous phrase, but a community founded on false premises.[64] And so it was with Griffith's film which, despite his defiant insistence that his film was true "in every vital detail"—he actually offered a large sum to anyone who could prove him wrong—was itself exposed to further research.[65] The thousands

64. Benedict Anderson, *Imagined Communities: Reflections on the Origin and Spread of Nationalism* (London: Verso, 1983).

65. D. W. Griffith, "Reply to the *New York Globe*, April 10, 1915, reprinted in Silva, ed., *Focus on "The Birth of a Nation,"* 79. For Griffith's use of historical sources and a detailed account of Griffith's deviations from historical

of pages of testimony published by the 1871 Joint Select Committee mentioned earlier, which Griffith used as source material, were revisited by historian Francis B. Simkins in 1927. Simkins regarded Dixon as a minor *romancier* overly impressed by Vergil, Camoëns, and Arthurian legends, and provided as a corrective an extended, brutally granular account that depicted Klan members as a mobocratic mass—generally slovenly, ignorant, ineffective, haggard, chaotic, oddly dressed, and widely distrusted. The Klan, he demonstrated, punished not black criminality but primarily voting, and attacked whites as well as blacks and women as well as men. They went after offenses such as selling liquor near a church or not obeying one's widowed mother. And on one occasion they forced a white man, a Negro, and the Negro's wife to "whip each other, and all three were forced to engage in filthy familiarities too lewd to publish."[66]

Armed with Simkins and other sources, those feeling the oppressive weight of the nation celebrated in Griffith's film could propose a more factual national narrative that did not begin with the chivalrous Klan. They could document the many means by which white America undertook to forgive, forget, and continue racial violence and injustice, all the while proclaiming ideals of freedom and equality. They could then offer a new narrative, supplemented perhaps by a fact of a different order drawn from the heart of the white fiction itself. Considered as an historical account, *Birth of a Nation,* they might say, may be no more than a white-supremacist fever dream; but considered as an indicator of the understanding and judgment of many white people at the time, the film is a document of unimpeachable integrity, a semi-voluntary and half-aware confession that

---

fact, see Stokes, *D. W. Griffith's* The Birth of a Nation, Chapter 7, "Griffith's View of History," 171–225.

66. Francis B. Simkins, "The Ku Klux Klan in South Carolina, 1868–1871," *Journal of Negro History* 12, no. 4 (1927): 622.

lays itself open to the judgment of a futurity it scarcely imagines but which is contained in its confusions, contradictions, and tensions, pointing in its way to a more perfect union than it is able to realize.

Nor is the film altogether lacking in historical accuracy, for it represents without apology or evasion what some would say is the essential experience of black people in America: they were brought here as slaves, they were liberated, they tried to exercise their rights as citizens, and they were attacked and killed by white people who blamed them for being so disunifying and whose claims to be acting in self-defense and/or on high principle were upheld by the nation's courts—and then they had to sit by and watch while whites glorified the entire process and themselves by producing artifacts like *The Birth of a Nation.* Since the consent of black people to the national amalgam had never been obtained or even sought, and since black people were never admitted into the national clan, these dissenting narrators of the nation might argue, a new story must be told that both grants black people a form of "national" status as a separate self-determining entity, and by this means, changes the story, which is to say the identity, of the entire nation.

This, at least, is one way of describing the general case made by Lee, Parker, and Miller, and also of some of those involved with "The 1619 Project," a collection of commentary, photography, poetry, and historical essays launched by *The New York Times Magazine* in August, 2019.[67] The premise of this project is that "the country's true birth date" is not 1776, 1781 (victory at Yorktown), 1783 (Treaty of Paris), 1787 (Constitutional Convention), 1790 (ratification of the Constitution), 1865, 1871, 1900, or 1915, and not even 1620, when the Puritans arrived on the Mayflower.

67. See *New York Times Magazine*, August 18, 2019, https://www.nytimes.com/interactive/2019/08/14/magazine/black-history-american-democracy.html.

Rather, the country was born a year earlier, when the first slave ship arrived at Point Comfort, Virginia.[68] This seems a remarkable and original claim until we consider that Griffith, too, begins his story with the arrival of slaves, the "disunion" long predating any notion of union. Griffith also anticipates the provocative claim by the 1619 project that the nation was founded on "a lie," with the only difference being that in *Birth of a Nation,* the lie is in the claim that "all men are created equal," while for the authors of the 1619 Project, the lie is in the assertion by the signers of the Declaration (one of whom was the great-great-grandfather of DuBose Heyward, author of the novel on which *Porgy and Bess* was based) that "we hold these truths to be self-evident," when their tolerance or defense of slavery demonstrated that they did not.[69] Griffith also anticipates the 1619 project in promoting a racialized, which is to say a biologized concept of the nation. The claim made by the project's leader Nikole Hannah-Jones that "anti-black racism runs in the very DNA of this country" represents a pseudo-scientific restatement of the sulfurous

68. "1619," *New York Times*, 13 August 2019, https://www.nytimes.com/2019/08/13/magazine/1619-project-livestream.html. The factual claims of the project, including the assertion that one of the primary motives of the American revolution was the protection of slavery, have been vigorously contested by historians. See for example Sean Wilentz, "A Matter of Facts," *Atlantic,* January 22, 2020, https://www.theatlantic.com/ideas/archive/2020/01/1619-project-new-york-times-wilentz/605152/. In 2020 the *Times* quietly dropped from the project's website the claim that 1619 was the "true founding" of the nation. But not quietly enough—the alteration was noticed, provoking a new round of attacks on the project. See Brett Stephens, "The 1619 Project," *New York Times,* October 9, 2020, https://www.nytimes.com/2020/10/09/opinion/nyt-1619-project-criticisms.html.

69. In the words of Nikole Hannah-Jones, the leader of the project, "The United States is a Nation founded on both an ideal and a lie." Essay in "The 1619 Project," https://www.nytimes.com/interactive/2019/08/14/magazine/black-history-american-democracy.html.

message steaming off *Birth of a Nation,* and suggests that racism is a heritable national legacy.[70] One could almost say that the 1619 Project was birthed in *Birth of a Nation.*

The thought that the United States was born as a slavocracy is distressing—an exemplary bad memory in Renan's sense—to any who really do hold those truths to be self-evident, but for those who wish to disturb the national self-understanding by offering a different story, 1619 represents an opportunity to improve on the pallid homogeneity of 1776, when all citizens, as far as the Declaration was concerned, were gathered into "one people." The premise of equality is hostile to narrative, which takes great interest in the particular and very little in the universal. Even the stylistically prosaic but dynamic, agonistic Constitution, populated as it is by sharply individuated persons—the president, vice president, electors, members of the Supreme Court, senators and representatives, Indians, on down to the shadowy region inhabited by those half-known figures, "persons bound to service"—is more compatible with narrative than the Declaration. Insofar as it is dedicated to the Declaration's principle of equality, the United States of America is narratively disadvantaged compared to sub-national groups that insist on their own particularity, some of whom feel that their claims to equality are being abrogated in practice, and whose interest in the Declaration is limited to the license it gives them to press their claims. Such groups, noting what Jefferson refers to in the Declaration as a long train of injuries and usurpations, can set about

70. This trope, which suggests the hopelessness of any merely social or political amelioration, is also used by Henry Louis Gates. His long-running PBS show "Finding Your Roots" performs genealogical research and DNA tests on mostly celebrity guests in an attempt to, as he puts it, "get into the DNA of American culture." Gates begins *Stony the Road,* his exhaustive study of Reconstruction and its terrible aftermath, with the statement that "anti-black racism" has "long become part of our country's cultural DNA" (xxii).

establishing themselves as virtual sub-nations with their own souls or spiritual principles by advancing their stories as compelling subplots within the large but shapeless national narrative. At the risk of creating some friction with other groups and with the nation at large, a group can promote its own vital, particular, interesting narrative as a more rewarding locus of identity than that offered by the vague, pale, smothering, and soulless fiction of universal equality and freedom.

The discovery of *Birth of a Nation* was that mass media can communicate a single visually and even viscerally compelling narrative fiction almost simultaneously to large numbers of people. In the end, this is Griffith's contribution to the theory of the nation, and to the nation. Viewers of his film sat together, transfixed before large screens, exposing themselves to a gigantic, visually and aurally stunning narrative that purported to represent the birth, the soul, and the story of the nation, learning simultaneously about history, the nation, and themselves.

It was of course a "Southern nation" that they were learning about, a nation dominated by the interests, values, and perspectives of a single region, with the part dominating the whole. This would probably have surprised Renan, who believed that that larger, pan-national entities would in due course swallow up nations—a European mega-state replacing the nations of Europe, for example—but did not anticipate any process by which a sub-group might erupt within the nation and claim for itself the kind of spiritual principle that founded national identity. But France was a far more homogeneous and organic nation than the United States, which, because of its size and complexity, was radically exposed to cyclonic frenzies of local self-assertion in which groups separated themselves from the national monoculture, withdrew or partially withheld their consent from the national fusion, and declared their semi-independence.

Semi-independence is built into the American system, beginning with the states, which, as Calhoun insisted, are in some respects more like nations than parts of a nation. But the possibilities for more specific affiliations based not on geography but on other principles have arisen from the nation's culture and history. Registering some disaffection from the federal nation, any of these possibilities is capable of organizing itself around a story that could be spread virally by technologies well beyond Griffith's imagining, birthing what are now generally called not nations but, *pace* Anderson, "communities"—the black community, but also the white supremacist, LGBTQ, Jewish, Asian, business, hearing-impaired, BDSM, cancer survivor, recovering addict, veteran, vegan, Hispanic, online gaming, and gun rights communities. Even people living on the streets in a state of total destitution are sometimes described as "the homeless community." By such means, disaggregated and disaffected groups of people can enjoy the oceanic sense of belonging associated with the nation without sacrificing the thrilling experiences of solidarity and resistance, even rebellion.

For better or worse, we owe the discovery of this potential to *The Birth of a Nation.*

2

SHOW BOAT AND THE STRAIN OF RACE

It doesn't seem possible that anyone ever had so
much sheer fun, gaiety, novelty, satisfaction
and money out of the writing of one piece
of work as I have had out of Show Boat.

—*Edna Ferber, A Peculiar Treasure*[1]

Like *The Birth of a Nation, Show Boat* is acknowledged to be a work of singular importance in the history of the art-form that spiraled out from its fertile example—in this case, that most American of theatrical inventions, the "integrated musical" in which dramatic and musical elements are placed in the service of character and narrative.[2] With a book written by Oscar Hammerstein based on Edna Ferber's 1926 novel, *Show Boat* opened on Broadway in 1927, the second show produced by Florenz Ziegfeld in his new Ziegfeld Theatre. Since then. *Show Boat* has been produced twice on film (1936 and 1951, not counting a half-talkie 1929 version very loosely based on the novel) and many times on stage, including several productions by opera companies, which generally treat it as an American classic.[3] *Show Boat*

1. Edna Ferber, *A Peculiar Treasure: An Autobiography* (New York: Doubleday, 1938), 263.

2. An early version of this chapter appeared in *Raritan*.

3. For a comprehensive account of all versions of *Show Boat* up to the mid-1970s, see Miles Krueger, *Show Boat: The Story of a Classic American*

may have begun its life upon the stage under the aegis of Ziegfeld, but it is now understood to be both a *summa* of American popular entertainment to that time and a transformative work that enlarged the artistic ambitions and deepened the moral seriousness of American musical theater. The transformative agent, the revolutionary element in a genre hitherto devoted to exuberant distraction, is what one reviewer described as the "racial subplot . . . a strain of urgent, unflinching commentary on the racial injustices of the post-Civil War South."[4]

Only rarely has the racial theme in *Show Boat* been treated as anything more than a powerful but ultimately subordinate element that gives the show a gravitas that deepens but does not alter the essential character of what Ziegfeld promoted as an "All American musical comedy" and "the grandest show you'll ever see." Concentrated in a few scenes at the beginning, the racial subplot is extended but trivialized in a subsequent blackface sequence, and then, in a development we will encounter again in the next chapter, apparently forgotten altogether as the action leaves the river and heads to Chicago, New York, and the twentieth century. The blackface performance in particular offends many, and each new production is greeted by accusations of racial stereotyping. Even those who applaud *Show Boat*'s moral aspirations often describe this scene as "insulting," "degrading," or even "painful." To defenders and critics alike, elements in the

---

Musical (New York: Oxford University Press, 1977). In 2020 Criterion released a Blu-Ray version that included, in addition to the 1936 film, excerpts from the 1929 version along with interviews and commentaries on various aspects of the film. They had originally been out of circulation from the mid-1940s until after the death of Paul Robeson in 1976.

4. Joshua Kosman, "S.F. Opera Review: 'Show Boat' a Riveting Slice of the South" *SFGate* (3 June 2014), http://www.sfgate.com/music/article/S-F-Opera-review-Show-Boat-a-riveting-slice-5523395.php.

show can be just as offensive as the practices and attitudes it ostensibly condemns.[5]

As long as the question of the show's endorsement or repudiation of racism is seen as the central issue, criticism will be frozen into tableaus of righteousness. But a different and more dynamic approach is possible, one that focuses not on the moral positions taken by the show but rather on the kinds of insights or recognitions it solicits, provokes, or enables. Most productively applied to the 1936 film, this approach views the show both as an historical artifact and as a stimulant for contemporary reflection on issues that, while urgent, resist conceptual clarity. The argument in what follows is that *Show Boat* is indeed an American classic, but only because the issue of race is not confined to a limited "strain," but informs the entirety from start to finish. In this reading, the second half of the film merely develops, according to a submerged but ruthless narrative logic, the implications of the first half. So far-reaching are these implications that the case can be made that *Show Boat* constitutes one of the most incisive and comprehensive representations of the social, historical, and ideological issues associated with race ever achieved in American popular culture, and stands as one of a very small

5. Comparing Langston Hughes's poem "The Negro Speaks of Rivers" with Hammerstein's lyric to "Ol' Man River," Todd R. Decker notes that Hughes's speaker "speaks in proper English" while Hammerstein "employs the black dialect of American popular song, slathering the most stereotypical pop culture blackness—should we say blackface?—all over the lyric." Decker does not state his criteria for "proper," but it is clear that in his view dialect does not meet them. Todd R. Decker, *Who Should Sing "Ol' Man River"? The Lives of an American Song* (New York: Oxford University Press, 2015). See also Warren Hoffman, "Only Make Believe: Performing Race in *Show Boat*," *The Great White Way: Race and the Broadway Musical* (New Brunswick, NJ: Rutgers University Press, 2014), 31–55.

number of artifacts in any medium that is at all adequate to the subject.

This case does not depend on authorial intention. There is little evidence that Ferber, Hammerstein, or Ziegfeld wanted to produce, thought they had produced, or indeed were at all capable of producing a complex, probing, or comprehensive representation of racial realities in America. Ferber, the daughter of a Hungarian Jewish storekeeper in Milwaukee, was a professional writer living in New York City, a winner of the Pulitzer Prize in 1925 for her novel *So Big.* Except for a view from a train when she was eight, Ferber had never seen the Mississippi River. But, having become excited through a chance conversation by the idea of a vanishing form of popular entertainment ("'What's a show boat?' I asked sourly. I'd never heard of them"), she researched the subject, interviewing people and reading up (*Peculiar Treasure,* 257). She was able to see a few performances of show boat entertainment on a boat docked in North Carolina, and wrote the novel in a year while living in a hotel in the Basque country. As a Jew, and as a determinedly single woman, Ferber was acutely sensitive to prejudice and discrimination. But neither the novel nor the rest of her biography gives evidence of a sustained attention to the problem of race. Near the end of her life, she told an interviewer that all of her novels were informed by a deep moral theme "except *Show Boat,* which hadn't any theme, which was just fun."[6] In her novel, the characters of Jo, as she spells it, and Queenie are minor figures. They work on the boat—she more than he—they horse around in amusing ways, and when the boat puts up for the winter they disappear, showing up in spring "penniless, in rags, and slightly liquored" (122).

6. Edna Ferber, interview, in Robert Van Gelder, *Writers and Writing* (New York: C. Scribner's Sons, 1946), 363; cited in Todd R. Decker, *Show Boat: Performing Race in an American Musical* (New York: Oxford University Press, 2013), 27.

Jo often sings, "a reedy tenor, but soft and husky with the indescribable Negro vocal quality" (121).

One of the novel's early readers, Jerome Kern, a Broadway veteran at forty-one, was taken with Ferber's accounts of the show boat's audiences, the "moving living drama of a nation's peasantry" filing in to see the show.[7] These audiences, Ferber's narrator said, sought simple emotions clearly expressed. They did not draw bright lines between life and art, they did not appreciate aesthetic subtlety or indeed any kind of subtlety, they did not hold their emotions in critical reserve. Kern saw in this concept the possibility of a multigenerational American epic that might appeal to urban audiences of the 1920s who were already nostalgic for the simple entertainments of an earlier day (the 1880s, when the novel begins), and prepared to be charmed by their own national history. He sold a reluctant Ziegfeld on the idea of a musical play that included black performers in significant roles, failed or unhappy marriages, and characters and situations closer in spirit to a serious play than to the annual "Follies" productions that had made Ziegfeld rich and famous, enabling him to build his theater. Recruited by Kern to write the book and the lyrics, Hammerstein immediately thought of casting Paul Robeson, not yet thirty but increasingly famous as a singer, actor, and presence in the Harlem Renaissance. Hammerstein grafted onto the minor figure of Jo elements suited to the outsized charisma of Robeson, producing a composite character of sloth and heroism, indolence and conviction, a bemused and self-absorbed indifference to the troubles of the world and a human monument to the quest for justice. Hammerstein never attempted to synchronize the character, and in fact subordinated the role to the actor, giving Robeson, in a 1928 London production, a suite of "Negro songs" in the middle of the production. Robeson would play the role in film and on stage until 1940.

7. Edna Ferber, *Show Boat* (New York: P. F. Collier & Son, 1926), 101.

Ferber's novel was, then, reframed twice by Hammerstein, first in the stage play and then, nine years later, in the Universal Studios film. For the film, Hammerstein and Kern made a number of cuts and alterations and added scenes and songs that exploited the skills and reputations of their veteran actors, many of whom had already played the roles on the stage, including Charles Winninger, Irene Dunne, Sammy White, Helen Morgan, and Robeson.

Although a thoroughly professional production of an established property, the film, like the novel, seems only half-able to understand itself on the subject of race. But a certain obliviousness, a self-forgetting or whiting-out that may be deliberate and determined, is a crucial aspect of the film's exploration of the subject. A more clear-eyed or consistent moral perspective might not have resulted in the depth or subtlety I am claiming for the film, which achieves its deepest effects when it seems least obedient to a single controlling creative intelligence and least responsive to the issues of justice, discrimination, or exploitation that have come to dominate critical discussion.

Beginning with Ferber's interviews and note-taking, authorial multiplicity and the importation, alteration, or reimagining of prior materials has always characterized *Show Boat.* Curiously, there is no official script of the show, so each revival is a reinvention conforming to contemporary sensitivities, with elements deemed unacceptable or disturbing removed or changed beyond recognition.[8] Hammerstein himself began the process. In the novel, Cap'n Andy is swept off the deck of the *Cotton Blossom* one night in a storm, his wife Parthy is a mean-spirited shrew from start to finish, the tragic Julie LaVerne ends up as a prostitute in Chicago, and Gaylord Ravenal is a compulsively self-destructive gambler who, after a chaotic boom-and-bust career in Chicago in which he and his small family careened,

8. See Krueger, *Show Boat*, 212–13.

sometimes in the middle of the night, from the Palmer House to the flophouse and back again, simply vanishes when his luck and money run out—all of which was apparently Ferber's idea of "just fun." None of this had made it onto Ziegfeld stage, but the Ziegfeld production had included a number that Hammerstein and Kern cut: "In Dahomey," in which black people performing as Africans at the World Fair were shown later talking about how they wanted to get back to their nice apartments after the performance. Considered problematic even in a show that featured blackface performers, this incident was left out of the film and has not been performed onstage since 1946.

For the film, Hammerstein, perhaps at Robeson's insistence, also removed the word with which his Ziegfeld production began, when a black chorus sings, "Niggers all work on de Mississippi." The unacceptable word has over the years been replaced with others less pungent but more palatable: "colored folk," "darkies," and "here we all."[9] In one 1966 production, the entire chorus was eliminated so that nobody at all worked on the Mississippi.[10] The word must have been at least striking in 1927, but by 1936 it was considered shocking and unperformable. Why did Hammerstein choose to begin with it? Neither carelessness nor insensitivity suffices to explain this decision. The only explanation is that the word bore a meaning he thought crucial to the whole.

9. The claim that Robeson protested the use of the word was made by Alberta Hunter, who appeared in a London production in 1928. See Will Friedwald, *Stardust Melodies: A Biography of Twelve of America's Most Popular Songs* (New York: Pantheon Books, 2002), 117. Friedwald points out that the black press at the time criticized Robeson for "singing 'nigger, nigger, nigger' before all those white people," adding, however, that the word is not found in any of Robeson's many recordings of the song. In his 1928 Brunswick recording, Al Jolson, who had made a tremendously successful career in blackface, used the word.

10. Krueger, *Show Boat*, 211–12.

The message is clearly that while slavery had been abolished, servitude had not, and that, for black people, manual labor under white bosses merely continued the relationship between the races that had officially been ended in 1865. Even with this perspective in mind, some commentators find it painful to hear the word "niggers" used by black people, even by actors, to describe themselves. When, in 1988, a complete and historic recreation of the 1927 production was attempted for a CD recording, the entire black chorus walked out rather than sing the first word, with the awkward result that the white chorus had to sing the parts allocated to the black chorus, beginning the show with the offensive word.[11] Hammerstein's motives have been explained in subtle ways, with some arguing, in effect, that the word is used with a sardonic tone that rebukes and defies the contempt built into the very language that whites used about African Americans. But this seems highly unlikely. There is no indication in this song, sung by people in the course of labor, of any clever undercutting or merely verbal subversion of the local power structure. The most plausible explanation is that Hammerstein saw this phrase as a customary usage of black people reflecting on the facts.

Those facts are given a more defiant and heroic articulation in the show's—and Hammerstein's—first great song, "Ol' Man River," which represents the moral core of the show, an anthem to honor the historical experience of black people in America that has seemed to many listeners to have the commanding authority of an authentic spiritual. The meaning is borne both by the song's lyric and by montages of men groaning under heavy burdens, toting barges (whatever that means) and lifting bales, tragic figures processing in leaden monotony, outlined against a darkened sky.[12] The staging owes something to the German

11. See Decker, *Show Boat*, 101–3; Ibid. 109.

12. Hammerstein admitted he had no idea how one might "tote" a barge. See Philip Furia, *The Poets of Tin Pan Alley: A History of America's Great Lyricists* (New York: Oxford University Press, 1992), 184–86.

Joe sweats and strains

Expressionist tradition the director James Whale (who had in the previous five years directed *Frankenstein, The Old Dark House, The Invisible Man,* and *Bride of Frankenstein*) sometimes deployed; as one critic noted, the bar that Joe staggers out of as he sings "Git a little drunk an' you'll land in jail" might have been frequented by Dr. Caligari."[13] The clear intention is to associate work on the river in the 1880s with slave practices in which black men were treated as beasts of burden by "de white man boss." So wretched is his existence that the singer contemplates self-destruction, asking to be shown the River Jordan that courses through many spirituals as the stream "dat I long to cross," the borderline between oppressive reality and a liberation most often achieved only in death. Black people in particular feel themselves intimate with the river, the song implies, because their long practice of survival has acquainted them with the futility of any protest about their condition and the deeply pragmatic wisdom of mere endurance.

What is often described as the "timelessness" of "Ol' Man River" reflects the lyric, which represents the river as a trans-human force of eternality and stoic endurance, and implies a continuum between slavery and post-slavery, as if the one simply flowed into the other. The setting of the song suggests both

13. Ethan Mordden, "'Show Boat' Crosses Over," *New Yorker* (3 July 1989): 81.

Lifting that bail

eras. Joe might be singing in the late 1880s, but the phenomenon of black laborers singing on the river was, according to Walter Johnson, one of the iconic images associated with slavery. In his study of the role of slavery in the economy and expansionist ambitions of the antebellum South, *River of Dark Dreams,* Johnson describes as a "racial-commercial sublime" the scene of grandeur and terror created by the spectacle of peoples, goods, machinery, and labor as slaves toiled, often at night by torchlight, loading and unloading the steamboats whose cargoes linked America to the global economy.[14] As the slaves worked, they sang. "What hidden force animated the spectacle of the singing slaves?" Johnson asks. "Was it the drumbeat engines and steam-whistle harmony of the steamboats by which their songs were framed? The rhythm of labor orchestrated by some purpose beyond their own? Or was it the evidence of some unfathomable kindred sorrow?" (82–83). This is the scene, and this the sorrow, evoked by "Ol' Man River."

So elemental and uncomplicated are the emotions unleashed by "Ol' Man River," so unanimous is the consent to its musical and moral greatness, that little would seem to be gained from a critical or skeptical approach, especially one that focused on the

14. Walter Johnson, *River of Dark Dreams: Slavery and Empire in the Cotton Kingdom* (Cambridge, MA: Harvard University Press, 2013), 83.

Joe gets a little drunk

audience response itself. But simplicity and unanimity suggest that the immense difficulties and complications surrounding the issues of slavery and race have somehow been smoothed over, and the question then becomes how and why this effacement has been achieved.

The place the effacement occurs is in the minds of the audience, and the key to the effacement is the very concept of intimated but suppressed knowledge that the song attributes to the river that "must know somethin' but don't say nuthin'." Every member of the audience—any audience—is in a higher social position than the singer of the song, who represents himself and all black people in the United States as victims of an injustice of historical proportions. This injustice both is and is not continuing: the singer, though black and poor, is a slave no longer, but a man capable of reflection and artistic expression who invites his listeners to feel an empathetic solidarity with him and those like him. The song itself throws out a line of communication and sympathy to the people in the audience, who are assured that their empathy, and their applause, will be received rather than flung back in their faces. Especially given this generous gesture by a man still feeling in his bones the effects of oppression, the audience is virtually compelled, in part perhaps by its own uneasy feelings of implication in the structures of discrimination and oppression to which the song testifies, to respond appreciatively, even ecstatically. To fail to do so would be to declare oneself indifferent to slavery, than which, for prosperous theater-goers, there is nothing more damnable. We know, we understand, and we condemn. So utter and unreserved is our contempt for slavery that we take shocked offense at individual words that recall it, no matter who, why, or in what context they are spoken. So refined are our sensibilities in this respect that we rejoice in the fact that the show we are watching is "integrated" both formally and in its casting, with black people sharing not only the stage but the spotlight; indeed, it is especially gratifying, for both historical and moral reasons, to be able to applaud the titanic rendering of black suffering by Robeson and his successors. Doing so, we align ourselves sympathetically with suffering humanity. We do not, of course, necessarily accept personal responsibility for that suffering, inflicted as it was by others long ago, and would resent any direct challenge or accusation, any suggestion that some serious adjustment in current arrangements was needed in order to right historical wrongs. But there is no such challenge because our hearts all beat as one. We deplore everything deplorable—if we did not, would the singer be singing to us?

This partial suppression of historical knowledge enables the general sentiment of warm approval that engulfs the singer, the song, and the audience at the end. Approval would be a difficult response to summon up if the singer were clearly the victim of brutality, or if the laborers surrounding him were in a state of rage or beaten into a cowering servility. But this is not the case. The first time Joe appears onscreen, a bare minute before he begins singing, he is transferring a sack of flour to Queenie's shoulders—Queenie, who berates him for being "de laziest man dat ever lived on dis river." Joe is not a slave at all—none of the black people is; they're all getting paid. Slavery has been assimilated to free labor, the brutal slaveowner to the unsympathetic boss, the slave past to the emancipated present. Yet Joe himself does not have any boss. He is barely employed on the boat, singing, loafing, shucking peas, and putting on a fancy costume to ride in the parade and sell tickets. When he sings about "you and

Joe's look of "grim but resigned suffering"

me" sweating and straining, he is whittling, to no apparent end. He ends the song with a beatific smile on his face, surrounded by his supporting chorus. (Hammerstein's script had called for "a look of grim, but resigned suffering," but Robeson, perhaps intuiting that this role would make him a movie star, had other thoughts.)[15] When Queenie berates him for his indolence, he replies in a song ("I Still Suits Me") filled with good-humored feminine rhymes ("I may be lifeless, / But wid one wife less, / My life would be mo' strifeless, yes siree"), and she ends up cuddling on his lap. They have, it seems, a very nice life. But lest we take a harsher view of Joe's indolence than Queenie does, Hammerstein creates an opportunity for heroism, sending him out on the river in a howling gale to fetch a doctor to deliver Magnolia's baby, which means that, with trees and craft crashing all around him, he rows upstream at least one way against wind, rain, and current—a magnificent, indeed impossible feat.

Joe may be, as Hammerstein's notes indicate, "a rugged and untutored philosopher," but he is far from a simple or even a coherent man.[16] The spokesman for black suffering and witness

15. See Decker, *Show Boat*, 153.

16. Oscar Hammerstein, *Lyrics* (New York: Simon and Schuster, 1949), 20; cited in Furia, *Poets of Tin Pan Alley*, 185.

to an historical tragedy of vast dimensions, he is also possessed of a large number of purely personal and oddly sorted characteristics, being lazy, fearless, powerful, indignant, resigned, proud, humiliated, self-indulgent, self-sacrificing, and given to gin. His sufferings at the hands of "de white man boss" are so great he thinks death might be preferable; on the other hand, his actual boss asks almost nothing of him, and he loves that boss and his family so much he will risk his life for them. What *is* Joe?

One way of making sense of him would be to think of Joe as a human incorporation of the encompassing metaphor of the river as described by Johnson in *River of Dark Dreams*. Johnson goes into astonishing detail in his descriptions of the ceaseless processes of conversion and transformation effected through slavery by and on the river. In countless ways, Johnson shows, black suffering was converted into cotton, which was then converted into profit, ease, and plenitude—the cherished "culture" of the South. In the course of this vast process, everything possible was turned to account. Nothing was wasted—not food (calories convert to slave energy), not bones (which fertilize the soil), not human or animal feces ("Manure is wealth," according to one farming manual). Even the raping slaveowner's semen, if it resulted in a birth, was thereby converted into capital.[17] Enabling trade, the river was both symbol and means of these conversions and transformations, to which "Ol' Man River" contributes some of its own: past into present, servitude into free labor, silent suffering into magnificent song, blank anonymity into smiling movie star, sympathy into applause, and audience indignation into self-satisfaction.

The river may withhold its knowledge, if it has any, but some people feel that at a deeper level they understand it. Ferber's novel includes many perfervid passages about the mighty indifference

17. "Manure is wealth": J. A. Turner, *The Cotton Planter's Manuel* (New York: C. M. Saxton, 1857), 57; cited in Johnson, *River of Dark Dreams*, 181. On the conversion of semen into capital, see Johnson, 196.

of the river as it slashes through human life on its self-directed course of creative destruction. But Ferber gives plangent and impassioned meditations on "The River! The River!" not to Jo, who evidences no interest in the subject, but to Magnolia, who was raised on the river and learned everything she knew about life from it and from the people she met on it. Indeed, at the end of the novel, after Parthy's death in 1926, Magnolia leaves her ambitious but soulless daughter Kim, who had taken singing lessons to try to learn what her mother had absorbed on the river ("there was no Mississippi in Kim") to her calculating climb up the show business ladder in New York, and returns to the show boat to end her days on the river (393). Accompanied by her polite but anemic husband, Kim visits the boat in an unsuccessful attempt to persuade her mother to leave the "flies and Negroes and mud and this yellow terrible river that you love more than me"; beginning her return trip to New York, Kim looks back and sees Magnolia on the deck, and the thought occurs to her that her mother is like the river, "eternal and unconquerable" (397, 398). Hammerstein appropriated this identification of person with river from the novel, but implied that it was part of the inherited sensibility of black people generally.

In fact, each race has its river. The "white" river embraces the color, variety, turbulence, and unpredictability of life, as well as commerce, vocation, and profit. Suggesting and creating opportunity, the white river is the mighty engine driving the American economy, American politics, American culture, and American intercourse with the world. The river gives mighty material form to the forces of fantasy and freedom; as Huck says, "You feel mighty free and easy and comfortable on a raft." For enslaved black people in the antebellum years, however, the river had different associations: the horror of being "sold down the river" or transported up the river to new owners, the chance of escaping slavery by swimming across it or secreting oneself on a boat heading north, and the possibility of shedding one identity midstream and adopting another on the other side. For those who could not manage to escape, the river offered a model of stoic indifference or the tantalizing possibility of oblivion, thoughts that, as "Ol' Man River" suggests, still visited black people years after the end of slavery.

The river divides the races but in a riverine version of miscegenation, also unifies them in a common recognition of the possibility of a universal fluidity, of transformation through exchange, concealment, or reinvention in which whatever is can be washed away, changed beyond recognition or simply obliterated. In a stroke of genius by Hammerstein, this capacity for an all-reconciling, all-effacing mutability is identified as suppressed knowledge, a silent understanding that resists or refuses articulation, an accepted truth that nevertheless cannot be spoken.

Partial suppression and half-concealment are at the core of the event that centers the first part of the film, the discovery of Julie's racial identity. This scene is the first of two in which, very briefly, black people are shown in acts of silent contemplation. Together, these scenes occupy just a few seconds of film; so quiet and unmarked are they that, especially considering the extraordinary action that surrounds them, we may overlook them altogether. But they exist, and attention paid to them is a legitimate part of a close reading of the film. The question in both cases is simple: What are these people thinking?

In the first of these scenes the local sheriff, who has been told of Julie's parentage by Pete, her spurned and vengeful suitor, charges the show boat's leading lady Julie LaVerne and her husband Steve with the crime of miscegenation. Having been warned of the sheriff's approach, Steve, in a plan obviously devised in advance for such an eventuality, had cut Julie's hand and sucked the blood in front of others, including the entire cast of players on the boat, as well as Joe and a crowd of black people who had gathered at the windows of the boat. This enables him to tell the sheriff that he has "Negro blood in him" and so cannot be guilty of miscegenation. The sheriff affirms that "in these parts," even "one drop" of Negro blood in a person condemns one and one's

Steve obtains black blood

heirs to all posterity to negritude in the eyes of the law and, if known, in the eyes of society. The taint was not always known, however, and so a light-skinned person such as Julie could pass as white; she could even marry a white man who was willing, as Steve was, to break the miscegenation law and to commit himself to assisting her—now their—risky practice of ongoing self-concealment.

Acquitted of the charge of miscegenation, of which they are actually guilty, Steve and Julie have now confessed to an offense of which they had not previously been suspected, the social crime of passing as white, although as everyone but the sheriff knows, only Julie has been passing as white, while Steve, as an accomplice to her passing, has been passing as a man legally married to a white woman when in fact he has been illegally married to a black one.[18] Now, with Julie's blood in his stomach, Steve has provided himself with the means of asserting that he has been passing as white all along, which means he is now, dishonestly, passing as black, although he can now also claim that his marriage is legal. Formerly an apparently white but in fact a

18. Anti-miscegenation laws were still on the books in several states until 1967, when the Supreme Court struck them down.

Steve and Julie leave the boat

mixed-race couple, they are now confessedly, if not actually, both black "in these parts." The two are now free to—and in fact must—leave the show boat because while, in the sheriff's mistaken view, they are not guilty of a crime, they have been committing a fraud that, if known, would shock the public so greatly that the safety of the couple could not be guaranteed.

It would be a mistake to think that Ferber had put all this together, or that she cared much about the subtleties. She had been told several versions of this story[19] during her year of research and had placed a version of one of them into a narrative whose center and main interest, for her, lay elsewhere. Hammerstein preserved the incident without seeming fully to understand its implications. But this brief episode is a thread that, plucked, unravels the fabric of race in nineteenth-century America, and regardless of what Ferber or Hammerstein thought or intended, drives the plot of *Show Boat* as well. And while neither Ferber nor Hammerstein gives evidence of reflecting on the incident once Steve and Julie leave the boat, others do. As the tragic couple departs, Joe, looking down from the balcony, his face captured from below in a closeup, bids a sorrowful goodbye

19. Julie Novkov describes this scenario as a "commonly reported romantic vignette of the era critical of the one-drop rule." See Novkov, *Racial Union: Law, Intimacy, and the White State in Alabama, 1865–1954* (Ann Arbor: University of Michigan Press, 2008), 146n.

Reflection

to "Marse Steve" and "Miss Julie," using their "white" names even though they are now, in different ways, both black. And as the pair pass from the boat to the shore, they walk through the crowd of black people who have just witnessed the scene with the sheriff. After the couple leave the frame, the camera lingers for a second or two on the people staring silently after them.

What are those people thinking? What thoughts are adequate to, or provoked by, the spectacle they have just witnessed?

They would understand that Steve and Julie have just been undone by having run afoul of race, the subject that has determined nearly everything about their own lives—what they are and do and have, as well as what they are not and cannot and have not. They would probably not have understood all the reasoning behind the white commitment to the notion that a great gulf divided the two races (except when, through rape, it did not), but they certainly felt the effects of that commitment every day. Such had been their experience, they might have felt themselves somehow to be different in deep and durable ways from whites. But they would also have understood the brutal reality of racial mixing, and would have seen cases like Julie's, where a person with black parentage attempted to claim an advantage by pretending to be white. They may have wondered why it required pretense to claim to be what one appeared to be, since color was supposedly the decisive phenotypical marker of race. They would, however, have understood without instruction the extreme social and legal consequences of a failed pretense, which would have added the offense of deception to the (parental) offense of crossing the barrier that separated the races.

Those who observed Steve and Julie's departure would in all likelihood have been uninformed about the immense intellectual apparatus that had been self-assembling over the course of the nineteenth century to delineate in scientific terms the racial characteristics of the Negro and to draw a bright line between white and black.[20] Biology had taken the lead, but other disciplines or proto-disciplines had followed. The famous passage in Thomas Jefferson's 1781 compendious *Notes on the State of Virginia,* in which he interrupts his discussion of inheritance laws with an extended rumination on the nature of racial difference shows how biology could slide into something like cultural anthropology. After venturing a number of learned but inconclusive speculations on the source of blackness in skin, Jefferson undertakes a list of distinctively Negro physical features and cultural behaviors, including a puzzling disposition to sleep, a "greater degree of transpiration," reduced secretion by the kidneys, greater secretion by the glands of the skin (leading to their "strong and disagreeable odor"), their own preference for the beauty of white people, a greater tolerance for heat, and a

20. On the historical origins of modern racial attitudes, see Winthrop D. Jordan, *White Over Black: American Attitudes Toward the Negro, 1550–1812* (Chapel Hill: University of North Carolina Press, 1968). Henry Louis Gates's *Stony the Road* is an invaluable resource for understanding the range and variety of white-supremacist thinking in both the general culture and in contemporary scientific discourse from Reconstruction through the Harlem Renaissance. On miscegenation, in particular, see pp. 136–41. See also Nicolas Bancel, Thomas David, and Dominic Thomas, eds., *The Invention of Race: Scientific and Popular Representations* (New York: Routledge, 2014). The essays in this volume are focused on what the editors call an "epistemological moment" between 1730 and 1790, when new ways of studying the human body and human variability resulted in the emergence of a scientific conception of race.

pronounced and unembarrassed lustiness that made males notably "ardent after their female"—the entire inventory suggesting that in general "their existence appears to participate more of sensation than reflection."[21]

Over the course of the nineteenth century, Jefferson's account of natural differences, in which he gave occasional evidence of a degree of sympathy for the cruelty of the situation in which black people found themselves in America, would be supplemented and refined by other researchers, who made observations about the Negro's lung capacity, faculties of smell and taste, body odor, the proportion of brain and nerves, cranial size and shape, and "facial angle." Still others contributed studies of behavior, noting the musicality, distinctive sleeping arrangements, work habits, and mating behaviors of black people. Couched in scientific terminology, such observations could acquire the status of scientific fact, as when, in one widely read volume, it was observed that, unless commanded by a white man, Negroes lapsed into a state of inertial "vegeto-animal existence."[22] But biology

21. Thomas Jefferson, *Notes on the State of Virginia*, Electronic Text Center, University of Virginia Library, https://web.archive.org/web/20080914030942/http://etext.lib.virginia.edu/toc/modeng/public/JefVirg.html, 265. Jefferson was not unsympathetic: he also noted that the "deep rooted prejudices entertained by the whites; ten thousand recollections, by the blacks, of the injuries they have sustained; new provocations [all of which] will divide us into parties, and produce convulsions which will probably never end but in the extermination of the one or the other race" were obstacles to coexistence (264). On Jefferson's views on slavery and black people generally, which are far more detailed, conflicted, and evolving than the few comments here can suggest, see Winthrop D. Jordan, *White Over Black*, Chapter XII, "Thomas Jefferson: Self and Society," 429–81. Black people held in bondage tested Jefferson's convictions about "natural and inalienable" rights. As Jordan notes "Jefferson's confusion at times became monumental" (453).

22. Quoted by Walter Johnson, *River of Dark Dreams*, 201. This phrase and others even more evocative are drawn from essays published in an

was increasingly the discourse to which arguments for racial hierarchy turned for scientific authority, as researchers of a less supple and self-complicating disposition than Jefferson lent their support to the view that the social differences between the races were merely proxies for organic factors that approached a species difference.

Not all thinking about race was scientific; many issues debated by scientists were worked out in practice, on the ground, in the moment. During the late 1880s, when the sheriff was confronting Steve and Julie, social practice and legal determinations were often based more on general social understanding than on empirical evidence obtained by credentialed professionals. At this time, as Peggy Pascoe points out, legal disputes about racial identity were typically settled by such factors as the church one went to, the associations one kept, parentage if known, the status one had in the community, or one's general reputation.[23] When identity was in dispute, courts accepted the testimony of neighbors, a practice the sheriff follows in accepting the testimony of those on the boat who affirm that Steve has "Negro blood in him." But the testimony itself, while unhesitating, unanimous, and effective—the sheriff accepts it as decisive—reveals a certain wobble in the concept. Blood is a fluid coursing through one's veins, but nobody would claim that if Steve's blood were to be examined his racial identity would be revealed. What the sheriff is asking people to testify to is their understanding of Steve's personal history, an understanding that can only have been learned from what people, including Steve, have said.

1860 anthology called *Cotton is King*, which Johnson calls "a *summa theologica* of pro-slavery thought." E. N. Elliott, ed., *Cotton is King and Pro-Slavery Arguments* (Augusta, GA: Pritchard, Abbott and Loomis, 1860).

23. Peggy Pascoe, *What Comes Naturally: Miscegenation Law and the Making of Race in America* (New York: Oxford University Press, 2009).

Why was blood the name for the crucial factor in deciding racial identity?[24] The answer must lie in the frictionless efficiency with which the term reconciles the empirical clarity of science and a folk belief, supported in the early twentieth century by the new discipline of eugenics, about the heritability of race and racial characteristics. Blood construed as what Julie Novkov calls "the bearer of blackness" was a biological name for a kind of difference that bore the most profound social and legal consequences but was in many cases impossible to identify or detect.[25] The difference between races was supposedly profound, but if a person (Julie) could resemble, behave like, and be accepted as a member of the other race—or if a person (Steve) could simply declare himself to be a member of a race he did not resemble and would not be accepted as—then what was race? *Where* was race? Was the racial difference merely subjective, or intersubjective, or even voluntaristic, or was there something more definite and substantial at work in establishing a distinction so crucial to one's life and the life of society? Blood was the answer to these questions, a seemingly literal term for a kind of difference that, while real, resisted literality.[26] Improvising without the advantage

24. At the time the *Cotton Blossom* was plying the river, a "blood fraction" or "blood-quantum" standard (often one-eighth) was commonly used in the South as the limit marking the boundary between black and white, so that a person with at least one great-great grandparent known to be entirely black was black in the eyes of the law. Blood quantum laws were originally developed by colonial governments beginning in the early eighteenth century in order to determine who was and was not Native American. They were not used by tribal groups until the 1930s, and then not by all groups, and not all in the same way.

25. Novkov, *Racial Union*, 118. For a subtle discussion of the intricate interplay between concepts of culture and race during the 1920s, see Walter Benn Michaels *Our America*, 110–23.

26. The philosopher Charles W. Mills has proposed, in this spirit, that race should be considered as a construction that is nevertheless often

of critical race theory, Steve had figured out that the merely metaphorical character of blood could not be acknowledged by those to whom the racial distinction was important given the work the concept was intended to do, and that if he ingested actual blood, he could claim to be ingesting race as well.

Over time, the increasing number of mixed-race people who appeared white began to complicate to an intolerable degree the clarity on which arguments for white supremacy depended. One response to the fear of racial pollution might have been to argue that the superior blood of the white race would ennoble and uplift the black race, and that given time miscegenation would solve its own problem.[27] The occasional social or professional success of mulattoes was indeed often attributed to their white blood, but this compliment to whiteness entailed an implicit acceptance of racial mixing, a fact not all whites were willing to concede. As Winthrop Jordan says in his discussion of the social management of interracial sex in *White Over Black,* the presence,

---

non-negotiable, a "*contingently* deep reality" (48) that possesses "social objectivity" (4) and is therefore both "real and unreal" (47). Charles W. Mills, *Blackness Visible: Essays on Philosophy and Race* (Ithaca, NY: Cornell University Press, 1998). The essay in this collection most directly pertinent to the present discussion is "But What Are You *Really?,*" which includes a probing discussion of ten cases of "racial transgressives," in which the various criteria—ancestry, appearance, experience, culture, and so forth—for racial identity do not align (49–66). The list could be expanded even further, as *Show Boat* demonstrates, for Mills does not include either blackface performance or any example of a voluntary surrender of privileged racial identity. See also Charles W. Mills, *The Racial Contract* (Ithaca, NY: Cornell University Press, 1997).

27. Writing in the third quarter of the twentieth century, Winthrop D. Jordan suggests that antebellum fears of black sexual predation on white women were unnecessary because "so far, a century and a half later, emancipation has actually lessened the rate of intermixture." Winthrop D. Jordan, *White Over Black: American Attitudes toward the Negro, 1550–1812*, 2nd edition (Chapel Hill: University of North Carolina Press, 2012), 542.

amounting to ubiquity, of mulattos undermined assertions of white supremacy and even of racial distinctions, and so, "by classifying the mulatto as a Negro [whites were] in effect denying that intermixture had occurred at all."[28]

The situation called for some nimble theorizing. Novkov describes one response that gained considerable currency in the South, the argument that while white *people* were superior in many ways to black people, white blood was for some reason powerless to defend itself against what Novkov describes as "an almost magical quality" in black blood "that enabled it to overcome white blood, even in the smallest quantities" (119). This was the rationale behind the desperate and extraordinary strategy—practically unique in the Western hemisphere—that became known as the "one-drop rule" (anachronistically invoked by the sheriff a generation before such rules actually began to appear).

The one-drop rule registered the panicked sense that a bright line had to be drawn, but as everybody knew, that line had already been erased by the very people now most concerned to draw it. And so, some realists, rather than pretending to a racial integrity in which nobody believed, devised other arguments that preserved the pride if not the purity of the white race. They resisted the incorporation of a one-drop rule into law because, as George Dionysius Tillman (brother of "Pitchfork Ben" Tillman, Governor and then Senator from South Carolina and a leading Klan supporter), said in a published 1895 speech,

> It is a scientific fact that there is not one full-blooded Caucasian on the floor of this convention. Every member has in him a certain mixture of . . . colored blood. . . . It would be a cruel injustice and the source of endless litigation, of scandal, horror, feud, and bloodshed to undertake to annul or forbid marriage for a remote, perhaps

28. Winthrop D. Jordan, *White Over Black*, 178.

> obsolete trace of Negro blood. The doors would be open to scandal, malice, and greed.[29]

Tillman was not saying that all men are created equal, a phrase that he, like many Southerners, regarded as a deeply unfortunate verbal blunder associated with the otherwise admirable Founding of the nation. He was simply acknowledging reality, and even proposing a justification, claiming that "the pure-blooded white has needed and received a certain infusion of darker blood to give him readiness and purpose." This claim, while necessary to avoid the implication that the white race had contaminated itself, carried the strange concession that the supposedly superior race had some deficiency that could only be supplied by the inferior race, and the even stranger implication that the qualities "received" were not those of sloth, stupidity, a bad smell, or ardor after the female (which was already manifested in the means by which the desired qualities were acquired) but "readiness and purpose," qualities that were in fact far easier to attach to the white rapist than to the raped black woman.

All this confusion was necessary for Tillman to be able to make his main case, that the races were in fact mixed to a certain degree (for good and honorable reasons!) and so racial identity could not be made contingent on an uncompromising standard of ancestral purity without blackening the entire white race, a consequence no white person could contemplate with equanimity. As printed, his speech carried a headline—"All Niggers, More or Less!"—that ensured wide readership

While compelling and even irrefutable, Tillman's arguments for a loose and liberal understanding of race were outweighed by the threat to the established but beleaguered order presented by miscegenation. By the end of the nineteenth century, as actual

29. George D. Tillman, "All Niggers, More or Less!" *Charleston News and Courier*, October 17, 1895, http://nl.newsbank.com/nl-search/we/Archives.

racial mixing proceeded apace and cases of passing proliferated, Jim Crow laws began to appear, all with the intended effect of asserting and ensuring the cultural and political supremacy of what Novkov, describing the prevailing concept in the South, refers to as the "consanguineous white race" (117). The "one-drop" or "hypodescent" laws that had their greatest impact during the time Ferber was writing her novel were part of this effort, and proceeded from the belief that the only way racial integrity could be maintained and white supremacy ensured was through a strict policing of the boundary between the races even if this meant offering up as ritual sacrifices laid on the altar of racial purity a few visually and culturally white people.

Even if the entire tangle of social and ideological forces responsible for driving Steve and Julie from the show boat was not immediately grasped by the black people who witnessed their flaming-sword departure, all of them would have understood that Julie was almost certainly the offspring of a rape, and that she, like Joe and Queenie and most if not all of them over a certain age, had spent her early years in slavery. They would also have understood that when the war ended, Julie, then a young girl, must have made the discovery that it was possible to make a new life by adopting white speech, wearing white clothes, displaying white mannerisms, marrying a white man, and learning white songs—while retaining the memory of the songs she had learned as a child, including "Can't Help Lovin' Dat Man of Mine." They could easily have inferred that Julie and her husband had determined to live a life of concealment and evasion, making the most of their skills in this field by becoming performers on the stage as well as in life. Julie's decision to pass as white would have been immediately comprehensible to those observing her departure; one improves one's position by any means possible, and any of them, if they looked like Julie, might have done the same. There was certainly no advantage in insisting on being black if one looked white, a fact that makes Steve's false admission of blackness, which purchases immunity from prosecution at the cost of a total loss of identity and reputation, admirable almost to the point of incomprehensibility.

Steve's admission, or rather assertion, was not altogether selfless. Both he and his wife were facing prosecution for the crime of miscegenation, or of the more commonly prosecuted crime of interracial fornication. But since the sheriff was, or permitted himself to be, persuaded that Steve and Julie had merely been passing, they are free to leave. Passing was not a crime but the concealment of a crime, one that benefited both the passer and his or her parents. Denying the mother and exonerating the father, the person who passed assumed the risk of exposure and its social costs while protecting the father from embarrassment, liability, responsibility, and prosecution. It was in the interests of white supremacy in the Post-Civil War era for mixed-race people to pass if they could.

Understanding the stakes involved in miscegenation gives us a richer understanding of why the safety not just of Steve and Julie but of the entire cast and crew of the show boat would have been in jeopardy if Steve and Julie had remained on the boat and their situation had become known. The show boat is a theater of desire, with Cap'n Andy touting Steve as "the handsomest leading man on the river!" and Julie as "the little sweetheart of the South—you all know how you all love her!" Another thing they all know, or think they know, is that Steve and Julie are white. If the white audience discovered that their erotic interests had been deliberately aroused and solicited for black people, they would feel not just misled but exposed. This would apply both to men and women, whose desire for black men was far more transgressive and insulting to the cause of white supremacy than that of white men for black women—rape being, after all, one expression of white supremacy. Both sexes would be legitimately enraged, and the show boat performers, as perpetrators of a cruelly mocking fraud, would feel the consequences.

Nolie gallivantin' around

In her personal and professional life, Julie is a magnet for the desires of white men, including Steve, her adoring audiences, and even the wicked Pete. Something of the same is true for Magnolia, who not only replaces Julie in the melodramatic theatrical performance of "The Parson's Bride," but also takes on another role fortunately never pressed on Julie. And here we come to the second moment of reflection on which I would like to dwell. As in the first, black people are shown in an act of observation and reflection that bespeaks an inner life that remains inarticulate.

Perhaps as a way to showcase the skill set of Irene Dunne, Kern and Hammerstein wrote a new song for the movie, a blackface cakewalk, "Gallivantin' Around," in which Magnolia performs as a young black woman, recounting the great time she had on a trip to Louisville where, as she tells her suspicious boyfriend, she was gallivantin' around ("my feet been offa the ground"), dancing and staying out late: "Ain't no tellin' all the times I fell in love and out again!" While Magnolia dances with a blackface chorus, the camera moves all around, focusing on her and on the audience in front of her, whites on the ground floor and blacks in the balcony. For a few seconds the camera ventures to the upper level, prowling around behind the black people, who are hunched over in close and silent attention to the

Two audiences

performer on the stage, knowing something, perhaps, but saying nothing, forcing us to speculate.

With a white woman describing and miming an exuberant and unapologetic black promiscuity, evoking an indiscriminate atmosphere of ardor of the sort that Jefferson observed in black men, "Gallivantin' Around" provides illicit thrills for everyone in the audience, awakening cross-racial desires in both men and women. The performance is invariably cited by critics of the show's representation of race. Todd R. Decker, whose *Show Boat: Performing Race in an American Musical* foregrounds the issue of race, is entirely in the mainstream in recording his discomfiture at this "troubling moment . . . an instance of extreme racial caricature that, together with Dunne's physically uninhibited shuffle in 'Can't Help Lovin' Dat Man,' marks this version of *Show Boat* with an embarrassing and extreme instance of Hollywood's depiction of blackness." Because of this, Decker says, the film as a whole "remains a document in racist caricature demanding careful historical explanation" (160). Decker actually approved of the fact that as of 2013, the public had been spared the pain he had experienced because the film had not been released on DVD (it was released the following year). And he is horrified by Hammerstein's original plan to have Cap'n Andy approach the camera during Magnolia's song and enjoin the movie audience to sing along. This, Decker notes, would have been "a stunning, perhaps disturbing addition" (160).

The view from the balcony

One would not wish disturbance on one's worst enemy, but notably, in the film, nobody is disturbed, much less stunned. On the other hand, the serious attention paid to the performance by those in the balcony suggests that nobody up there could be described as entertained either, although they did pay to see the performance. Something else is happening. Let's try to think it through.

The balcony audience is undoubtedly aware, first, that while white people could portray black people, the situation could never be reversed. Joe could never sing "Ol' Man River" on the *Cotton Blossom*; and even forty years later, a mixed-race cast acting in a musical play that involved both races (Ziegfeld's 1927 *Show Boat*) was an unprecedented and perhaps for some disturbing novelty on a Broadway stage. Miming the other race—like "make-believe" generally, to note the title of the song Magnolia and Ravenal sing on first meeting—is, in *Show Boat,* the prerogative of white people.[30] (Indeed, as the removal of "In Dahomey" for the film suggests, by 1936 black people could not even be depicted imitating black people without causing problems.) Hammerstein himself had appeared in blackface in a production

30. Ziegfeld's production did not have a blackface performance like "Gallivantin' Around," but it did have an "actual" blackface performer, an Italian American actress from Wilkes-Barre, Pennsylvania, Tess Gardella (who later performed as Aunt Jemima), in the role of Queenie.

of the Columbia University Varsity Players in 1916. In *The Great White Way: Race and the Broadway Musical,* Warren Hoffman comments bitterly that only white people in *Show Boat* get to make believe while blacks are constrained to live in obdurate biological reality, or "forced to perform in circumscribed roles that whites have defined for them."[31] Hoffman cites Michael Rogin's *Blackface, White Noise,* which argues that blackface consolidates white racial identity by demonstrating that the blackness of the white performer can be deliberately applied, then washed off, while whiteness is ineradicable.[32] In all these ways, we are told, blackface represents a racial insult by the triumphant white race, an act of casual contempt worsened by being passed off as light entertainment.

But the specific content of the pretense must be noted as well as the general insult. Among the things white people can pretend is that the "natural" behavior of black people can be mimed and mined for entertainment, and that black people themselves are reducible to caricature. This is a lesson people will evidently pay good money to be taught. Disappointed that the film does not undertake what Hoffman calls a "more radical dismantling of black racial stereotypes," many white critics of a later era have noted that blackface anticipates subsequent appropriations or translations of black culture by Paul Whiteman, Elvis Presley, Ricky Nelson, the Rolling Stones, and countless others (35–36). The injustice of such appropriation might have been less apparent, or less interesting, to the balcony audiences of the late 1880s than the demonstration that white people could imitate and make faces, a skill widely believed to be a peculiar aptitude of

31. This argument is made by Hoffman, *The Great White Way*, 41.

32. See Michael Rogin, *Blackface, White Noise: Jewish Immigrants in the Hollywood Melting Pot* (Berkeley: University of California Press, 1996). On the use of blackface by black performers, see Arthur Knight, *Disintegrating the Musical: Black Performance and American Musical Film* (Durham, NC: Duke University Press, 2002).

black people. (The dangers of cultivating a skill at pretending, as demonstrated by the disastrous unraveling of Ravenal's performance as "a Ravenal, of the Tennessee Ravenals," are less widely noted, but may have been intuited by those in the balcony who, like Joe, have "seen a lot of folks like him on the river.") In 1933, some forty years after Magnolia's fictional performance, Zora Neale Hurston would write in "Characteristics of Negro Expression" that "the Negro, the world over, is famous as a mimic . . . He mimics for the love of it. . . The average Negro glories in his ways. The highly educated Negro the same . . . the art of mimicry is better developed in the Negro than in other racial groups. He does it as the mockingbird does it, for the love of it."[33] Magnolia's performance demonstrates that white people can do this too. Fascinating. But the thought that white people could not only imitate, but imitate black people may have been interesting for another reason as well.

Most black people may have been constrained to be black, but the fact that white people could imitate black "ways" suggests that blackness could be assumed, performed, and applauded. This recognition might have stirred up the thought that the faculty of imitation in which, like mockingbirds, black people glory just for the love of it might be turned to other purposes than household amusement. If white performance of blackness constitutes the height of privilege, power, and freedom, perhaps a performance of whiteness—as in passing, or, more broadly, just acting as if you had status and worth—might be empowering as well. For black people, such performance has its risks, as Julie discovers, but also its rewards for those who could pull it off. Perhaps everyone and everything is imitable. Perhaps, in that respect, we are, in Tillman's phrase, "all Niggers"—more or less.

33. Zora Neale Hurston, "Characteristics of Negro Expression," in Nancy Cunard, ed., *Negro: Anthology Made by Nancy Cunard, 1931–1933* (London: Nancy Cunard at Wishart & Co., 1934), 57.

The applauding whites in the audience could hardly be unaware of the blacks in the balcony—they lived in close proximity, and entered and left the show boat on the same gangplank. There was apparently a general bi-racial agreement that blackface performance did not seriously damage the interests of either group. The attitude of silent, serious attention displayed by those in the balcony suggests that, far from feeling insulted or freshly aggrieved by Nolie's performance, the black people in the audience found it not just inoffensive but suggestive, worthy of thought. Perhaps . . . perhaps the blacks in the audience—who, if "Ol' Man River" is to be believed, were not altogether content with their lot—might be glimpsing in Magnolia's performance the lineaments of a different ordering of things, in which they enjoyed a greater share of the world's bounty, a richer array of opportunities for fulfillment and self-realization than they could at present. The sight of someone making a living, a good living, by imitating them might have been, at some level, in some way, illuminating. Perhaps some might even have glimpsed in such a performance the distant approach of a Scott Joplin, a Bert Williams (who worked in blackface), a Bill Bojangles Robinson (who did not), or even a Paul Robeson, commanding the respect and admiration of an international audience by performing, and even—in a sense—by performing blackness. Seeing themselves as others saw them, the balcony audience may have approached the realization that they might be seen and valued for something other than their labor.

It is also conceivable that some in the balcony, looking to have a good time, actually enjoyed seeing themselves represented in a manner to which they had become accustomed as entertaining, gifted people, and enjoyed thinking that their behaviors were actually considered interesting and valuable even if they themselves were not.

And, too, they might have been aware, even in their little river town, of the turbulence of Reconstruction, ended just a decade ago, which had placed black people in the U. S. Senate and House of Representatives, with murderous responses from the White League and the Klan who exercised what they regarded as their right and privilege of self-defense. Considering all this, perhaps some in the balcony might have reflected that it would not be an altogether bad thing if white people thought of them as a docile labor force when working and as idlers indulging their natural inclinations to singing, dancing, and gallivantin' when not working. Yes, let them think that.

To focus on the pain suffered by morally fastidious contemporary white viewers at the sight of racial stereotypes is to miss all this.

Consider in this rich speculative context the moment when Magnolia discovers her talent for imitation. She and Julie are in the kitchen, and Julie, explaining her love for Steve, begins to sing "Can't Help Lovin' That Man of Mine." Queenie comes into the kitchen and expresses surprise that Julie, a white woman, knows that song, which is apparently sung only by black people. Julie, both alarmed at the near-discovery of her secret and irritated by the suggestion that she doesn't know the song, starts up again. The melody itself seems bi-racial, beginning with "white" intervals in "Fish gotta swim, birds gotta fly," but diving into a bluesy flatted note with "*lov*in' that man of mine." Joe enters and declares that to be "my fav-o-rite song." Then, in a sudden and amazing transformation, Magnolia begins slopping around the kitchen in what Hammerstein's stage directions for the play describe as a "coon shuffle," a ridiculous loosey-goosey parody not directly of black people, but of white pantomimes of black idiocy and shiftlessness.[34] Queenie and Joe are vastly amused, as they surely would not be if they felt she was imitating or ridiculing actual black people, and the moment when Magnolia

34. Cited from Hammerstein's unpublished 1927 script, lyrics, and book of *Show Boat* in the Flo Ziegfeld-Billie Burke Papers housed in the Billy Rose Theatre Division, New York Public Library for the Performing Arts, in Hoffman, *The Great White Way*, 46.

Nolie breaks into a "coon shuffle"

and Queenie both burst into laughter at the performance is the most unforced and untheatrical moment of human affection in the entire film. The black people on the shore are also hugely amused—a white person is whitefacing the blackface, parodying the parody!—and Magnolia leads Julie, Queenie, and Joe out to the deck, where all four finish this "Negro" song (about a woman's helpless devotion to an unworthy male) as if it were a show-stopping theatrical performance.

Magnolia's ability to mime blackness is discomfiting to scholars today, but it entertains audiences and eventually saves her. When Ravenal leaves her stranded in Chicago, she seeks employment at the only trade she knows, an episode Ferber represents in far greater detail than Hammerstein. In the novel, Magnolia presents herself to a producer as a singer of "Negro songs" that she had heard by being around river boats, bayous, and landings, and of course Julie. Expecting something in the "Hello, Mah Baby" mode, the producer is surprised and disappointed when Magnolia sings spirituals. Still, he is struck by a quality—"Voice and—I don't know—way you sing. . . Your voice sounds like a—ain't that the truth?" He encourages her to learn some "real coon songs" and return for another audition.[35]

35. The "coon song," often merged with the syncopated rhythms of ragtime, was a staple of turn-of-the-century vaudeville, and then of Ziegfeld's annual Follies. Sophie Tucker began her career as a "coon shouter,"

They finish the performance

She buys a banjo, refines her presentation, gets the job, and rises and rises. This would not have been possible if her artless performance had not been thought to capture some dimension of the human condition that was, in the white world, rare, valuable, and meaningful even to those who could not fully comprehend it. Many years later, Sam Phillips of Sun Records in Memphis would be saying, "If I could find a white boy who could sing like a black man, I could make a million dollars."

Hammerstein misses this point. In his script, it is Julie, played by Helen Morgan, who draws together the Trocadero cast as well as the janitorial and wait staff in silent admiration for her soulful rendering of "Bill"; Magnolia is hired only when she demonstrates to a skeptical manager that she can "rag" "Can't Help Lovin' That Man" at frantic quadruple time. This makes for a comical scene but does not explain why, when she actually does perform on New Year's Eve, she is singing "After the Ball," which is neither a coon song nor a rag, but the kind of sentimental late nineteenth-century ballad that coon songs and rags had driven from the stage.[36] Hammerstein understands the

---

and Al Jolson, whose biggest success came in blackface with "My Mammy," made his Broadway debut in 1910 in blackface singing "Paris Is a Paradise for Coons" (lyric by Jerome Kern). See Furia, *Poets of Tin Pan Alley*, 25–37.

36. "After the Ball," written in 1891 for an amateur minstrel show in Milwaukee, became Tin Pan Alley's "first million seller," according to Furia, *Poets of Tin Pan Alley*, 47.

difference between that elusive and alien "quality" and hopped-up caricature, and the difference between "Deep River" and "Mistah Johnson, Turn Me Loose." But by eliminating the scene in which Magnolia impresses the show's producer by her rendering of spirituals, he misses the opportunity to mark the role, or the possibility, of a good-faith rendering grounded in experience, sympathy, affection, and respect, in the white mediation of black culture.

Having taken this wrong turn, the film blunders on. Magnolia's vast success over the next twenty years produces the phenomenal amount of money that drives the plot to a happy ending. Kim is making her Broadway debut to a packed house of the cultural and social elite. Magnolia and her parents, Parthy and Cap'n Andy, years removed from the river and show boats, are arriving late, their ocean liner from London having been delayed by fog. A police escort—are they heads of state?—gets them to the theater just as Kim is beginning her performance. At the same time, Magnolia's husband Ravenal, who has returned from years of itinerant destitution to work incognito at the theater so he can be near his daughter—who for some reason doesn't recognize him with a mustache—is standing outside the private box to which the late arrivals are escorted. Parthy, in a full-length mink and heavy jewelry, and Cap'n Andy in black tie and top hat—they clean up amazingly—enter the box, but Magnolia, following, spots her husband. No hard feelings, the couple reconciles instantly and she invites him into the box. Cap'n Andy is delighted to see him; Parthy gives a sniff but does not throw a fit.

Then we see the performance. It consists of mincing, bleached, sissified versions of "Can't Help Lovin' That Man" and "Gallivantin' Around." First a tropically picturesque group of black dancers, or rather, blacked-up white dancers—not obviously representing Southern slaves, with bare chests and straw hats suggesting some Caribbean setting, but what else could they be?—prance around before yielding the stage to couples of

Kim (center) on Broadway

antebellum belles and beaux, who twirl in cotillion fashion. Kim does some solo twirling. She does not sing—this twirling is the whole act. When it ends, the crowd is rapturous with delight. Out for an encore, Kim directs the audience's attention to "another Ravenal in the house," her more famous and now-retired mother, and suggests that Magnolia sing her old favorite, "You Are Love," which she had first sung on the river with Ravenal. Magnolia obliges. Ravenal, who had been discreetly creeping away down the hall, hears the song and, touched by this ancient memory, starts singing too. Magnolia hears him, and, announcing that there is yet another Ravenal in the house, invites him back into the box, where they sing together. The crowd erupts with cheers and applause at this unexpected abundance of Ravenals. Everyone is rich, famous, and forgiven.

Then, abruptly, a final shot of the Mississippi, and Joe's voice: ol' man river just keeps rolling along. All this nonsense was Hammerstein's invention.[37]

37. As the author of the film's book, Hammerstein bears the responsibility but did not conceive the ending in precisely this way. As Miles Krueger notes, Kim's performance was originally far more elaborate, beginning with Kim's singing "Gallivantin' Around" as an *homage* to her mother and the showboat tradition before the stage revolved to reveal a set depicting a downtown nightclub on stage right. Here Kim would lead dancers through fox trots and rhumbas, and a far more animated club in Harlem

Nolie and Gaylord reunited

This blindingly white ending seems designed as a way of consigning the issue of race to a "strain." But is it not possible to be outraged at this degrading depiction of white people, this ignorant caricature, this slandering stereotype? Hammerstein is asking us to believe that at the very peak of Broadway, when over two hundred shows were performed each year at seventy theaters—when Ziegfeld himself was in the middle of his fantastic run of "Follies," that had featured such stars as Josephine Baker, Fanny Brice, Eddie Cantor, Sophie Tucker, Bert Williams, and W. C. Fields; when the Theatre Guild was staging Dorothy and DuBose Heyward's *Porgy* with an actually rather than cosmetically all-black cast; and when the Harlem Renaissance was in full swing, with Duke Ellington packing them in at the Cotton Club—audiences would have roared in appreciation for Kim's vacuous but vicious antebellum pantomime.[38] In

---

on the left, so that, as Krueger says, Kim could "announce that the public has now seen her mother's song performed both the old and new way" (*Show Boat*, 147). The extreme length of the film as shot demanded cutting, and the final version of the ending, which Krueger regards as coarse and trivial, is the result.

38. In 1927, the year of Kim's performance, Ziegfeld's Follies starred Eddie Cantor and featured music by Irving Berlin, including "St. Louis Blues,"

fact, those audiences were roaring for *Show Boat*, but this is not that kind of show, nor even the kind of show that *Show Boat* made obsolete—it's a kind of show that had never been feasible on Broadway, whose audiences demanded more entertainment than Kim could have provided. Both Kern and Hammerstein reportedly despised "You are Love," which may be Hammerstein's must stunningly banal lyric, an extraordinary deflation in a show that contains "Ol' Man River."

Then why did they end it this way, showing white audiences such a deeply unrealistic and unflattering image of themselves? Once again, speculation is necessary. Perhaps Hammerstein simply wanted to end on a positive note and required success and reconciliation in all directions—and a fine memory of Robeson's voice—to achieve this. An interpretation more complimentary to Hammerstein's seriousness, subtlety, and social conscience would be that he wanted his audiences both to experience the bliss of a happy ending and to be indicted by their own pleasure when they recalled that all that success had been built on the foundation of the black culture Magnolia absorbed on the show boat, of which one drop, but certainly no more, may remain in Kim's desiccated performance. Perhaps Hammerstein wanted to register the fact that, as well intentioned as it may have been, Magnolia's translation of that culture had made possible and perhaps even inevitable further dilutions in which the historical experience from which that culture had grown was conveniently forgotten. By depicting a genealogical progression from the historical tragedy of slavery to the cultural disaster represented by Kim, Hammerstein may be forcing on his white audiences a recognition of the true character of the relentlessly extractive process by which whites have always, in America, wrung pleasure, profit, and entertainment from black suffering.

"The Jungle-Jingle," and "Shaking the Blues Away," the last sung by "Ruth Etting with the Jazzbow Girls."

Perhaps he wanted to confront his audiences with the hard truth that the logical terminus of the sequence of events inaugurated by the rape that begat Julie—not of course the beginning but somewhere in the middle of a much larger process—is the elimination of black people altogether.

Would Hammerstein think that he could escape the implications of his own narrative? Could he claim with any credibility that his own creation was a different species from Kim's? Or does his conclusion—a final return to the still-rolling river and to Joe's now-disembodied voice singing the last few notes of "Ol' Man River"—imply an accusation of all those, beginning in this case with Ferber but including Kern, Ziegfeld, Robeson, and himself, who have discovered how to profit from an imitation or representation of a black culture that remained largely unable to profit from itself? If this is Hammerstein's intent—to jab a splinter of reflection into our heels as we twirl on—then he is not just critiquing but mocking the culture that so richly rewards the Kims of the world, and that would, he surely knew after opening night in 1927, also reward him and everyone else involved in what Ziegfeld called this "All American musical comedy."

3

PORGY AND BESS AND THE *DANSE AMÉRICAINE*

"*Porgy and Bess* is not just great songs. It is a moving story about the citizens of Catfish Row."

—*Audra McDonald, introducing the HD performance by the Metropolitan Opera, 2019*

The problem with black people who leave their homes in the South to go north, according to one source, is that, in their eagerness to realize their full human potential as individuals, they sacrifice the security and the deeper sense of belonging that comes from membership in a tightly knit community bound by common experiences, shared traditions, and mutual responsibility. Able to go anywhere, such people soon discover that they belong nowhere; they arrive in the new place only to find that they are out of place, estranged from others and even from themselves. They acquire opportunities and shed a history of oppression, but they no longer know who they are. Or, as that source —Maria, who runs a cook-shop in Catfish Row in DuBose Heyward's 1925 novel *Porgy*—says, "De fus t'ing dat dem nigger fuhgit is dat dem is nigger."[1]

They are not the only ones. Forgetting and remembering play strong roles in accounts of American identity and citizenship,

1. DuBose Heyward, *Porgy* (Jackson: University Press of Mississippi, 2001), 50.

especially those such as Michael Walzer's "What Does It Mean to Be an 'American'?" that are based primarily on the immigrant experience.[2] In his widely admired 1990 essay, Walzer sketches out two competing accounts of American citizenship. In the first, or "pluralist" account, Americans live a hyphenated existence in which some vivifying memory of a homeland is retained even in the new country to which they have come. For Italian Americans, Chinese Americans, Mexican Americans and others, civic or public life, along with all broadly ideological or political issues, are pushed over to the right side of the hyphen, leaving all the sources of private happiness, including language, customs, communal celebrations, and traditions on the left. For these groups, America offers the benefits and opportunities of a liberal and tolerant polity but remains a principle of citizenship not belonging. The label of "American" serves only, as Walzer puts it, as "a dull protective coloring" that must be balanced by other, more emotionally satisfying sources of identity (39). Unlike other nation-states, the American state is not a *patrie* or a "homeland." Americans "have no inwardness of their own. They look inward only by looking backward" to the organic communities they left behind. The state itself is "anonymous," and America is "an anonymous nation of named nationalities" (41). The crucial fact, for theorists of the pluralist persuasion, is that Americans are free to retain as much as they wish of their old communal identities, free "to remember who they were and to insist, also, on *what else they are*" (28). In the words of a popular song written by the sons of an immigrant, "The memory of all that—no, no, they can't take that away from me."[3]

In the second account sketched out by Walzer, America does in fact possess a robust national identity, but, unlike other

2. Michael Walzer, "What Does It Mean to Be an 'American'?" in *What It Means to Be an American* (New York: Marsilio, 1992), 21–49.

3. "They Can't Take That Away from Me," music by George Gershwin, lyrics by Ira Gershwin (1937).

nations, it is one based not on language, ethnicity, or genealogy but rather on a recognition of a common history and a commitment to certain political or ideological principles. Citizenship, in this "republican" account, confers a civic, as opposed to an ethnic or cultural identity in which everything on the left side of the hyphen is a kind of crutch to be used only until the citizen no longer needs it. And ultimately, one does not need it, for everything that one might need and want resides on the right side, in the ideas of liberty, equality, and republican political principles, all protected by what Max Weber described as the "rational-legal authority" of American civil society.[4] Abstract though they may be, these principles can sustain a genuinely satisfying and even spiritual life; to be an American can be just as fulfilling and enriching as to be anything else. The symbols of public identity such as the Pledge, the Flag (and, more recently, perhaps, the Wall), which seem to pluralists to be devoid of positive content, are, properly considered, more than sufficient to ground a rich and substantive American political identity. The American state, according to this theory, is far from anonymous, and in fact works to efface the identities that people brought to the country and to overwrite them with Americanness. "Republican" theorists think time is on their side, as more and more people come to consider themselves natural-born Americans. If the pluralist account stresses the role of voluntary and partial forgetfulness, the republican account emphasizes a process Walzer describes as "mental erasure" ending with "absolute forgetfulness" (27).[5]

4. According to Weber, the rational-legal authority is one of the three types of authority with a claim to legitimacy, the other two being "traditional" and "charismatic." See Max Weber, "The Three Types of Legitimate Rule," trans. Hans Gerth, *Berkeley Publications in Society and Institutions* 4 (1958) 1: 1–11.

5. Quoted in Walzer, *What Does it Mean*, 27. The quotation is from Horace M. Kallen, *Culture and Democracy in the United States* (New York: Boni & Livewright, 1924), 138.

In an elegantly evenhanded solution, Walzer splits the difference by saying that, contrary to both schools of thought, Americans are free not only to preserve the hyphen but to choose which side of the hyphen they prefer, and even to switch back and forth between culture and citizenship as one's mood changes or the occasion warrants. As the immigrant's ethnic identity fades, the center of gravity will inevitably migrate to the right, strengthening the republican side of the ledger; but with new arrivals coming all the time, pluralism keeps gaining new recruits. Sustained by this alternation between pluralist and republican principles, more a constantly renewed rhythmic pulse than a steady linear progress in one direction, American society is, Walzer says, "radically unfinished" and productively incoherent (48). Indeed, Walzer says, American politics "*needs* a certain sort of incoherence" in order to remain open, dynamic, and creative (49). With the Constitution being silent on the question of citizenship, this chronically unfinished and unresolved quality is, for Walzer, the essence of "what it means to be an American": the freedom to choose your identity, with the assurance that the nation will support your choice.

Walzer's essay displays many of the "American" virtues it celebrates, being informal in manner, confident in tone, and egalitarian; it is both respectful of cultural difference and pragmatic about the need for points of commonality. But it is also exposed to the charge that it is itself "unfinished" in that it fails to engage with or even allude to the actual experience of immigrants. Classic works such as Jacob Riis's *How the Other Half Lives* (1890), Upton Sinclair's *The Jungle* (1906), Herbert Asbury's *The Gangs of New York* (1927), or Anzia Yezierska's *Bread Givers* (1925), as well a vast number of narratives both fictional and non-fictional about Chinese, Italian, Jewish, Swedish, Irish, and other immigrants tell a darker story of hardship, exclusion, hostility, discrimination, and violence directed at newcomers. One response to Walzer might, then, begin by posing simple questions: Has the laborious, dangerous, and emotionally wrenching process of shedding an old identity and making a new one in America typically been driven by a love of freedom and equality? Do people generally leave their homelands in a spirit of free choice; do they leave with intense regret at the loss of a rich and sustaining traditional culture? Once landed, do they then set about determining the timing, manner, and degree of their assimilation? Or is the immigrant experience more characteristically driven by hunger, poverty, war, persecution, and general lack of opportunity in the old country, and greeted by different forms of the same in the new country, to which are added nativist bigotry, exploitation, and a bewildered sense of lostness, all of which persist until the immigrant gets to the point where, his position being somewhat more secure and his residual differences somewhat less conspicuous, he can perhaps begin to think about making the choices Walzer describes? In short, does not the emphasis on the *meaning* of Americanness threaten to eclipse a more urgent subject, the actual *experience* of becoming American? And, for that matter, might there not be more meaning in that experience than in any set of concepts, propositions, or distinctions?

Thirty years after it was written, Walzer's meditation on American identity seems an artifact of a kind of Golden Age, not of immigration but of theorizing about American identity and citizenship, a time when the nation as a whole was more respectful than it is today, in the third decade of the twenty-first century, of immigrant desires and aspirations, more prepared to accommodate newcomers on whatever terms they preferred, more willing to offer and to secure the conditions they required in order to make new lives. Today, a generation after 9/11, the forces arrayed on the right side of the hyphen have grown more powerful. A Department of Homeland Security has been created, sporting events have become more manifestly patriotic, international agreements have been weakened or canceled, the geography and even the concept of war have expanded in disturbing new ways, and public support and governmental resources have been mobilized on behalf of a long list of anti-immigrant measures.[6] The freedom to forget or remember an older organic culture is now pressured on all sides. From the left comes the insistent suggestion that immigrants should insist on retaining vivifying memories of their previous culture as a principle of identity and resist becoming flattened into generic Americans; from the right, a demand that they pledge unquestioning allegiance as a condition of acceptance.

But to return: was it ever the case that the American experience, as opposed to American rhetoric, was characterized primarily by freedom? According to the historian Gordon Wood, equality was, in the early years of the Republic, by far the more attractive, comprehensible, and consequential concept—"the most radical and most powerful ideological force let loose in the Revolution."[7] In the first giddy years of the Republic, Wood says, the abstraction of freedom was largely ignored by citizens, who, on being told that they were equal with all others in the new political world, scrambled to establish some definite position. Many found that the shortest path to status or prestige was through wealth, a marker of worth that did not contradict the principle of personal moral equality. For Wood, the American

6. In the words of a widely circulated political slogan during the Trump administration, America sought to become "great again," which is to say, more "finished" and "coherent." President Trump himself said that the reason for his extremely restrictive immigration policies was that "the country is full." Quoted in Zeke Miller and Jonathan Lemire, 'Our Country is Full': Trump Says Migrants Straining System," *AP*, April 6, 2019, https://apnews.com/d604da469caf44fb854fd05a67ee15d7. The person in the Trump administration most responsible for formulating those policies, Stephen Miller, wrote that, "America without her culture is like a body without a soul. Yet many of today's youth see America as nothing but a meeting point for the cultures of other nations." Quoted in Jonathan Blitzer, "Get Out," *New Yorker* (March 2, 2020): 46.

7. Gordon S. Wood, *The Radicalism of the American Revolution* (New York: Vintage Books, 1991), 232.

innovation lay not in the promotion of liberty, but rather in a new intensity of competition and, inevitably, in ever-harsher forms of inequality and unfreedom. With freedom and equality disambiguated, the former shriveled to inconsequence and the latter became twisted into a general conviction that the measure of a man was determined by the weight of his purse—"a kind of equality," Wood notes, that "no revolutionary had ever anticipated" (243).

The absence of and indeed indifference to freedom in a society ostensibly dedicated to it was a striking anomaly, especially in the eyes of foreign observers. De Tocqueville regarded the neglect of freedom and the triumph of equality as a disease of democracy that "sinks deeply into every corner of the human heart, expands and fills it entirely . . . a burning, insatiable, constant, and invincible passion."[8] And Hannah Arendt noted that an early concept of political freedom, or "public happiness," was, in the early decades of the Republic, replaced by "private happiness" in forms available only to "an inward domain of consciousness" as the enlightened citizens envisioned by the Founders devolved into self-interested individuals concerned only with acquisition and consumption, activities she describes with some contempt as "the ideals of the poor."[9]

To his credit, Walzer seems uneasy with his own facility in arranging a solution that seems, as he notes, to "accentuate the positive," to make everybody happy, citizens and theorists alike (42). The sign of this disquiet is a tendency to place in parentheses anomalous or resistant elements that defy his own generalizations. Immigrants came to America by choice, Walzer says, "(except for the black slaves)"; or, "America has been, with severe but episodic exceptions remarkably tolerant of ethnic pluralism

8. Alexis de Tocqueville, *Democracy in America*, trans. Gerald Bevan (New York: Penguin, 2003), 297, 586–87.

9. Hannah Arendt, *On Revolution* (New York: Penguin Books, 2006), 130–31.

(far less so of racial pluralism)."[10] A whole series of invisible or silent parentheses interpolate themselves into Walzer's argument about what it means to be an American, for blacks did not come voluntarily, their former culture was not available to them for public celebrations, they did not retain their language, they were not in most cases able to form families much less recall their own genealogies. As chattel, they were already "anonymous" as far as the state was concerned and long before there was a state; and even after Emancipation, pluralistic tolerance for new immigrant groups, such as it was, was not extended to them. Until and even after the passage of the Civil Rights Act and the Voting Rights Act in the mid-1960s, racial discrimination in varying forms prevented black people from becoming full Americans in the republican sense, joining with others in the celebration of freedom. Other groups could eventually choose to blend and become entrepreneurs of life unencumbered by their origins, but black people retained their history in their skin. (In an irony that has not gone unnoticed, the national identity of white immigrants, who, however pressed by circumstances, chose to come to the country, can be traced back to an act of individual volition, while that of blacks, who came to the country en masse and enchained, is hereditary, non-voluntary, and collective—an altogether thicker and deeper form of belonging, if not of citizenship.) In an account of American identity centering on the act of forgetting, Walzer effectively forgets blacks.

Not altogether, though: in a footnote, he concedes that "a historical and empirical account of the place of blacks in the 'system' of American pluralism would require another essay, a different book" (45).

In fact, that book had already been written, although not as a single volume, and not as theory. I am referring to George

10. Michael Walzer, "Pluralism: A Political Perspective," in *What It Means*, 60; and "What Does It Mean," 44.

Gershwin's 1935 "folk opera" *Porgy and Bess,* with libretto by DuBose Heyward, whose novel was Gershwin's source and inspiration, and lyrics by Heyward and Ira Gershwin. Routinely described as the greatest and, with the exception of Virgil Thompson's 1934 *Four Saints in Three Acts,* the first true opera written by an American, *Porgy and Bess* has been widely discussed both for its purely artistic achievement—"the highest creative achievement in American classical music,"[11] according to one authority —and for its treatment of race. On both points controversies have been so intense that other possibilities for critical understanding have been neglected, among them the issue I wish to raise here, the possibility that the opera can be understood as an extended, multi-dimensional meditation on American identity. Never directly engaged in the work itself, that meditation occasionally comes into tantalizing near-focus, as in the comment cited at the beginning of this essay in which Maria describes bluntly as an illusion the belief of those who leave Catfish Row for the urban life of the North that they can also leave behind their history and prior identity. Her larger points, cast in the terms of Walzer's discussion, are that identity is not so easily shed or invented, that an "American" anonymity is not always achievable, and that if you try or pretend to forget who you are the world will find ways to remind you.

In what follows I will treat *Porgy and Bess* as an effort to imagine what American identity would look like if we removed the parentheses and actively remembered what is always in

11. Joseph Horowitz, "*Porgy and Bess* at the Met," *The American Scholar* October 9, 2019, https://theamericanscholar.org/porgy-and-bess-at-the-met/#.XlqiX5NKhao. Thomson's opera had a libretto by Gertrude Stein (which Gershwin described as producing "the effect of a 5-year-old prattling on"), and like *Porgy and Bess*, an all-black cast. Gershwin, letter to DuBose Heyward, 26 February 1934; quoted in Howard Pollack, *George Gershwin: His Life and Work* (Berkeley: University of California Press, 2006), 150.

danger of being forgotten if not repressed in theoretical or general accounts. By beginning on Catfish Row, we set aside both of the options Walzer describes, a hyphenated American identity with emotional and cultural life residing on the left side of a hyphen, and a more unified un-hyphenated civic identity organized around political or ideological commitments, neither of which was available to black people living in Charleston, South Carolina in the early years of the twentieth century. Starting on Catfish Row, we come immediately rather than eventually or reluctantly to other neglected factors in the formation of American identity—hard necessity rather than freedom, constraint rather than choice, losses rather than gains, and exclusion rather than either pluralist or republican citizenship. Above all, we begin with experiences of injustice, discrimination, deprivation, and violence that have always been part of the American story and that were suffered in extreme and prolonged forms by the descendants of slaves. On the principle that the anomaly may provide a better guide to the rule than the norm by introducing the larger category that includes them both, we begin by treating black people not as exceptions to a general rule but as hyperclarified instances of that rule, and as the most revealing indicators of what it means to be an American.

From the very beginning of his career, Gershwin had the ambition of giving musical voice to the American national character. As early as 1920, at the age of 22, he spoke of his desire to write "operettas that represent the life and spirit of this country . . . appealing to the great majority of our people."[12] He described

12. Gershwin, quoted in "Tales of Tin Pan Alley: 'Swanee' and Its Author," *Edison Musical Magazine* (October 1920): 9. Isaac Goldberg quotes Gershwin as saying that he wanted to interpret "the soul of the American people." Isaac Goldberg, "Childhood of a Composer," Robert Wyatt and John Andrew Johnson, eds., *The George Gershwin Reader* (New York: Oxford University Press, 2004), 35. These pages are excerpted from Goldberg's *George Gershwin; A Study in American Music* (New York: Simon &

Rhapsody in Blue (1924) as "a musical kaleidoscope of America"; the following year, he appears to have decided that a comprehensively and authentically American piece of music should be based on Negro music—a "Negro opera," as he put it, centered on and performed by black people, "almost a Negro 'Scheherazade.'"[13] "I shall write it for niggers," he said. "Blacks sing beautifully. They are always singing; they have it in their blood. . . . There will probably also be a nigger orchestra."[14] Gershwin believed that the heart of American culture was its music, and that the music with the strongest claim to indigeneity was the music

---

Schuster, 1931). Gershwin notes that "the greatest single racial influence upon American music as a whole has been that of Negroes," but points out that black music is itself "an agglomeration of many influences in its own history" (49). In his extremely interesting 1939 Harvard Bachelor's thesis, "The Absorption of Race Elements into American Music," Leonard Bernstein used Gershwin as his primary example, describing him as a "conservative composer" who undertook the "small and thankless" task of symphonizing jazz by appropriating Negro scales and rhythms. Leonard Bernstein, *Findings* (New York: Simon & Schuster, 1982), 54.

13. "Musical Kaleidoscope," Gershwin, cited in Isaac Goldberg, *George Gershwin: A Study in America Music* (New York: Frederick Ungar, 1958), 139. "Negro Scheherezade," Gershwin, quoted in Henrietta Malkiel, "Scheherazade in West Virginia: Jazz Opera on Its Way," *Musical America* (April 25, 1925): 3, 26.

14. Gershwin quoted in Herbert S. Greenhalgh, "When We Have Jazz Opera: An Interview with Mr. George Gershwin," *Musical Canada* (October 1925) 13–14. In using the word "nigger," Gershwin may have been referring to the usage of Carl Van Vechten, author of the novel *Nigger Heaven* (1926), and at that time Gershwin's choice of librettist for his proposed opera. In *Nigger: The Strange Career of a Troublesome Word* (New York: Pantheon Books, 2002), Randall Kennedy wrote of Van Vechten that he "had shown time and again that he abhorred racial prejudice. . . . It was against this backdrop of achieved trust that [Langston] Hughes (and other black writers) rightly permitted Van Vechten to use *nigger* as so many African Americans have used it—as an ironic, shorthand spoof on the absurdity of American race relations" (53–54).

produced by black people, a large and various category including jazz, ragtime, and spirituals.[15] In the year, 1925, that Heyward published his novel, another book appeared that Gershwin might have read with great interest: *The New Negro,* the influential anthology of writings centering on the Harlem Renaissance edited by Alaine Locke, who said in the introduction that "a genius that would organize . . . [the] distinctive elements [of Negro folk song] in a formal way would be the musical giant of his age."[16] The following year, Gershwin read Heyward's novel in one spellbound sitting and felt immediately that the story, set in a richly musical culture that reached back before jazz or ragtime, lent itself to opera, with its tendency to de-realized or

15. As Wilfred Sheed says, Gershwin "must have brought just about every black pianist in Harlem home to his apartment at one time or another, and to hell with the landlord's opinion." Sheed, *The House that George Built with a Little Help from Irving, Cole, and a Crew of about Fifty* (New York: Random House, 2007), 66. Gershwin's sense of the role in American culture played by black music expands on the claim of W. E. B. Du Bois that black "sorrow songs" were "the sole American music." W. E. B. Du Bois, "The Sorrow Songs," *The Souls of Black Folk,* in W. E. B. Du Bois, 357–547 in *W. E. B. Du Bois Writings,* ed., Nathan Huggins (New York: Library of America, 1986), 536. In the same essay, Du Bois also argues that black culture is distinguished for its "gift of story and song—soft, stirring melody in an ill-harmonized and unmelodious land" (545). See also W. E. B. Du Bois, *The Gift of Black Folk: The Negroes in the Making of America* (New York: Oxford University Press, 2014). In an interview with an American newspaper in 1893, the Bohemian composer Antonin Dvorák, whose "New World" symphony was largely based on spirituals, predicted that "Negro melodies" would foster an "American school" of operas, symphonies, and art songs. Quoted in Joseph Horowitz, *"On My Way": The Untold Story of Rouben Mamoulian, George Gershwin, and* Porgy and Bess (New York and London: W. W. Norton & Company, 2013), 26. On other developments that brought black material onto New York stages, see Horowitz, 25–28.

16. Alain Locke, "The Negro Spirituals," in Alain Locke, ed., *The New Negro* (New York: Simon & Schuster, 1997), 209.

exotic settings, stylization, magnification, and emotional intensification. He wrote to Heyward, who had also contemplated an operatic treatment of his novel, and proposed a collaboration, which Gershwin then deferred until 1934 while he prepared himself for the enormous task. In those seven years, Gershwin wrote many of his most famous songs, including "I Got Rhythm" (1928). And in addition to writing more than one entire show a year he was beginning to write a number of musically sophisticated and ambitious works, including the "Second Rhapsody" and "Variations on 'I Got Rhythm.'" Somehow, he also undertook intensive studies of harmony, counterpoint, composition, and orchestration. Finally, his studies completed to his satisfaction, Gershwin spent several weeks in 1934 in Heyward's company, living on Folly Island near Charleston, South Carolina, visiting churches and listening to local speech and music. Over the next nine months, he produced the piano and vocal score for his opera, the published version of which runs to five hundred and sixty pages, and the orchestration, which in manuscript contains seven hundred pages.[17]

The Gullahs to whom Gershwin was listening were culturally, historically, geographically, and even linguistically distinct, anomalous even among African Americans. Gullah people had been brought from the central western region of Africa—entire tribal communities had been plucked from Angola—to the Low Country in the eighteenth century, primarily to work in rice fields. Laboring in relative isolation from white people on large

17. These details are offered by DuBose Heyward himself, "Porgy and Bess Return on Wings of Song," *Stage* (October 1935), 28. On Gershwin's lifelong musical education, much of it with eminent teachers, see Pollack, *George Gershwin*, 38–40; Ibid. 118–56. Pollack also suggests that Gershwin was acquainted with Gullah music long before his 1934 visit because he had attended high school in the San Juan Hill area in the West 60s of New York. The black population there included many Gullahs, who had a direct influence on the stride pianists the young Gershwin knew well.

rural plantations, they managed to preserve more of their African traditions than other slaves, and developed their own creole dialect.[18] By the end of the nineteenth century, the plantation culture having collapsed, many Gullahs and slaves from other parts of South Carolina had moved into cities such as Charleston. Heyward's Gullah characters lived in a tenement whose picturesque ruination testified to the city's post-war economic decline. With the possible exception of Peter the honey-man, none among Heyward's characters was old enough to have been born a slave, but some had relatives who worked as paid servants in the city's homes where their parents and grandparents had worked as slaves, while others worked as vendors, on the docks, or as itinerant seasonal laborers. The first sentence of Heyward's novel sets the action in a "Golden Age," but the Catfish Row he describes is beset by violence, prostitution, poverty, and drugs.

The word used on Catfish Row to describe the common condition is "nigger," a term that describes with brutal efficiency a state of being that resists assimilation into the American mainstream, and which one ignores or forgets not just at one's peril,

18. For the West African origins and distinctive isolation and durability of the Gullah culture of South Carolina, see Peter Wood, *Black Majority: Negroes in Colonial South Carolina from 1670 through the Stono Rebellion* (New York: Alfred A. Knopf), 1974). In *The Souls of Black Folk*, W. E. B. Du Bois describes the overpowering strangeness of the local population to the Northerners who, in 1861, after the Union captured the islands off the coast of South Carolina, went south to help the freed slaves become self-sufficient. Encountering Southern slaves for the first time "face to face and heart to heart," the Northerners must have been amazed at what they found: "black folk of primitive type, touched and moulded less by the world about them than any others . . . Their appearance was uncouth, their language funny, but their hearts were human and their singing stirred men with a mighty power." Du Bois, *The Souls of Black Folk*, in *W. E. B. Du Bois Writings*, 537. For Gullah history, see William Pollitzer, *The Gullah People and Their African Heritage* (Athens: University of Georgia Press, 1999).

but at the cost of any grip on personal identity and social reality. To be a nigger on Catfish Row is to be part of an intimate and supportive community, but it is also to be at the mercy of circumstance, exposed to violence and chance, perpetually at a disadvantage in the larger society, and almost without support or resources in case of emergency other than those provided by others like oneself. The hurricane that damages the city devastates Catfish Row; the contracts that bind all signatories bind niggers cruelly; the law that protects all citizens threatens the citizens of Catfish Row with sudden and capricious incarceration. At one point, Heyward's characters break out into a song that must have drawn Gershwin's attention: "Ain't it hahd tuh be a nigger . . ." (68). To be a nigger is hard in itself, and hard in that it amplifies, aggravates, or accelerates any other vulnerability one may have, so that life is reduced to constant calculations of immediate necessity. When Porgy comments on the suddenness with which two women whose partners died in a hurricane attach themselves to other men, Bess says, "Dey is diff'rent fuh true. An' yuh won't never onduhstan'. All two dem gal gots baby fuh keep alive. Dey is jus' 'oman an' nigger at dat. Dey is doin' de bes' dey kin—dat all" (148). All the injustices and inequalities of what Walzer calls the American "system" converge in a single word, or, in this case, two words.

The Gullah community was distinct within the population of Charleston, but in several respects, the community described by Heyward shared a number of features with other immigrant communities; indeed, in a 1932 essay on "The Negro in the Low-Country," Heyward invited his readers to "consider the Negro, not as a human chattel to be bought and sold, but as an immigrant arriving out of an old world to take his place in a new and strange one."[19] The "saucer-burial" of Robbins, around which

19. DuBose Heyward, "The Negro in the Low-Country," in James M. Hutchisson, ed., *A DuBose Heyward Reader* (Athens: University of Georgia Press, 2003), 35.

Gershwin built the monumental "My Man's Gone Now," exemplifies the kind of solidarity and altruism that can sustain a stressed and traumatized group of recently arrived citizens. The resistance to turning over to the authorities one of their own even on a charge of murdering a member of their community testifies not only to group loyalty but also to the vast emotional distance between that group and the authority of the state. Even Gullah speech seems a compromise between English and some other language, as if the creolized new language had only been half-mastered or an older one only half-forgotten. The opening lines of the play as originally performed in New York in 1927 were, "Enty yuh yeddy huccum Porgy' ma done title um 'cause dat' nigguh nyam tummuch fish?"[20] The line demarcating Gullah from white was in some ways clear and bright; and yet, the Gullah people were not altogether outcast from mainstream white-dominated culture. They lived—sometimes on the same block—and worked among white people in private homes, on the streets, and on the docks, where Heyward himself had labored. With whites far less prosperous than in former times and blacks employed as free labor, the racial divide, while still

20. According to Dorothy Heyward, the intention—almost immediately abandoned—was to begin the play in Gullah but moderate into a more recognizable Southern African American speech. Dorothy Heyward, "Porgy's Native Tongue," *New York Times,* December 4, 1927, https://timesmachine.nytimes.com/timesmachine/1927/12/04/96682754.html?pageNumber=207. Of particular interest is Peter Wood, "Gullah Speech: The Roots of Black English," Chapter 6 in *Black Majority*, 167–91. Wood describes Gullah speech as the result of a "pidginizing process" that began in West Africa, where captured black people from separate regions had to blend their languages as best they could while awaiting deportation. Many slaves, Wood points out, encountered French, Portuguese, Spanish, and even Arabic before coming to America, along with English. Over the course of the nineteenth century, South Carolina Gullahs were increasingly isolated from white people, and so their English deteriorated as the dialect grew stronger.

profound, was bridged by a network of individual relationships that suggested a general acceptance on both sides of a principle of coexistence. Heyward's biographer suggests that the "sense of privation, of something lost that could never be regained," constituted a link between black and white in Charleston that enabled "the imaginative leap of feeling" that resulted in Heyward's sympathetic account in *Porgy*.[21]

Like other immigrant groups in the first years in the new land, the Gullah community in *Porgy* stands ambiguously inside and outside an American culture that tolerates but does not welcome it. Members of such groups may try to undertake the "mental erasure" Walzer says is entailed by republican citizenship, to surrender some of the signs of difference that had at first sustained and exposed them; they may try to "fuhgit dat dem is nigger" in the interest of having more political power or social capital. But if they succeed in that forgetting, they stand to lose something precious. They may, like the urbanized pimp and drug dealer Sportin' Life, trade their impoverished but reassuring communal identity for a life of crime and social marginality that only places them in permanent jeopardy from the law and other hostile powers. And even if they somehow find a way into mainstream culture, they may be suspected of merely feigning anonymity and concealing a private, ecstatic alliance with the old community and the old ways. They may be suspected of having merely donned the "dull protective coloring" of Americanness, while secretly retaining—in the closet as it were—the more gorgeous tonalities of their former lives. They may be denied respect or status, for reasons that remain maddeningly unstated. All immigrant groups are vulnerable to these suspicions and their consequences. And so, while the pigmentation of the deeply and multiply marginalized Gullahs marks

21. James M. Hutchisson, "Introduction," *A DuBose Heyward Reader*, ed. James M. Hutchisson (Athens: University of Georgia Press, 2003), xix.

them in a way different from other immigrant groups, all those who come to America from elsewhere are marked, and exposed, in some way.

Some aspects of Heyward's depiction of Gullah culture spoke to Gershwin directly. Gershwin had grown up in the polyglot lower East Side of Manhattan, his family part of a Jewish culture defined, like the Gullahs of Charleston, by ethnicity, language, religion, and heritage. Like many Jews, Gershwin felt an affinity with black people on the basis of a shared history of exile and persecution, and even current treatment. His family, like that of Irving Berlin and many others living on the Lower East Side, had fled Russian pogroms to come to America, where they found, as Wilfred Sheed puts it, "American black people not only singing about a similar experience, but using the Hebrew Bible as their text."[22] One of Gershwin's friends recalled that "George saw blacks and Jews as being the same in relation to the rest of society."[23] Even at the height of his fame, Gershwin was occasionally turned away from hotels.[24] He deeply admired black music, in which he heard not only energy and invention but certain chromatic resemblances to Hasidic melodies. What one writer called "the curiously sagging quality—so typical of Jewish art" had an echo in jazz, which, Gershwin

22. Wilfred Sheed, *The House that George Built*, 9. Sheed notes that Berlin was discovered at sixteen as a singing waiter in a Chinese restaurant called "jarringly, Nigger Mike's" (15). It is worth pointing out that Gullah people also read the New Testament. See the translation done by the Sea Island Translation Team, *De Nyew Testament* (The New Testament in Gullah) (New York: American Bible Society, 2005).

23. Emily Paley, speaking in 1987, quoted in Joan Peyser, *The Memory of All That: The Life of George Gershwin* (Milwaukee, WI: Hal Leonard Corporation, 1993), 132.

24. On a 1934 tour to celebrate the tenth anniversary of *Rhapsody in Blue*, Gershwin had been refused accommodation at a hotel in Toronto. Peyser reports a similar incident at Lake Placid, NY (*The Memory of All That*, 132).

claimed, was "not Negro but American."[25] A few years before he wrote *Porgy and Bess,* Gershwin had attempted an operatic setting of S. Ansky's Yiddish drama *The Dybbuk;* this was never completed, but a number of his songs, including many in *Porgy and Bess*—"My Man's Gone Now," "Oh, Bess, Oh Where's My Bess?," "What You Want wid Bess?" and "Gone, Gone, Gone" —definitely "sagged." "I Got Plenty o' Nuttin'" is essentially a translation into operatic Gullah of the sentiment—that poverty did not entail destitution, and that fulfillment did not require wealth—defiantly asserted by Ethel Merman in Gershwin's 1930 show *Girl Crazy:* "I got rhythm . . . who could ask for anything more?"[26] In adulthood, Gershwin enjoyed the acquaintance of a

25. Constant Lambert, *Music, Ho! A Study of Music in Decline* (New York: Charles Scribner's Sons, 1934), 211. Intending to discredit both black people and Jews, Lambert argued that jazz was predominantly a European creation, as proven by the facts that "at least ninety per cent of jazz tunes are written by Jews," and that African natives reportedly prefer Russian folk songs to jazz (211). See also George Gershwin, "Jazz is the Voice of the American Soul" (1925), in Wyatt and Johnson, *The George Gershwin Reader*, 90. See also Gershwin, "Our New National Anthem" (1927), 92–93. On jazz as a Tin-Pan Alley adaptation of Negro music, see Pollack, *George Gershwin*, 46–60.

26. The director of a highly controversial staging of the opera at the American Repertory Theater in Cambridge, MA in 2011, Suzan-Lori Parks, said of this song (which was renamed "I Got Plenty of Nothing"), "That's the song that folks will go, 'Oh man that's a racist song,' you know, it's basically the happy darkie with the empty pockets song.'" Quoted in Andrea Shea, "*Porgy and Bess*: Tweaking a Classic for the 21st Century," WBUR News, August 18, 2011, https://www.wbur.org/news/2011/08/18/porgy-and-bess. To solve this problem, Parks staged the scene in a way that indicated that by "nothing," Porgy was referring to excellent sex with his new girlfriend Bess. However the first Porgy, Todd Duncan, said the impression that "Plenty o' Nuttin'" was "a buffoon song" was the fault of the singers, not of Gershwin, who intended the song to be "bitter." "The Porgys that I've heard," Duncan said, "really don't know who Porgy is. They've not gone into the depth of who the character is." Interview with

remarkable range and number of people; an index to any Gershwin biography is a comprehensive list of the eminent people of his day both in America and in Europe. His extraordinary talents were almost universally recognized and honored. The same could not be said for most, or indeed any black people at the time, but Gershwin's fame and wealth did not prevent him from feeling that he understood, almost from the inside, black music and, through that, black culture.

Gershwin was uncompromising in his rejection of one of the dominant forms of black-Jewish rapprochement in the field of entertainment, the use of blackface.[27] He refused the suggestion made by the Metropolitan Opera that the regular Met singers appear in blackface, and, insisting that the black characters be played by black actors, took his show to the Alvin Theatre instead. And he supported his cast in 1936 when they refused to perform at the National Theater in Washington until the policy of refusing admission to black people was suspended.[28] But to some, the color of the cast signified not decisiveness but confusion. A review in *The New Republic* suggested that the "trouble with the whole thing" was that it was "neither black nor white." The cast, the reviewer thought, needed "to be darker or made up so."[29] This unusual suggestion was in one sense part of

---

Robert Wyatt, 1990, reprinted Wyatt and Johnson, *The George Gershwin Reader*, 224.

27. The most famous of the Jewish blackface stars, Al Jolson, sought to secure the film rights to *Porgy* before Gershwin began work on his opera. He also planned a blackface production of a silent film, with music by Jerome Kern and book by Oscar Hammerstein II. Fortunately for all involved, the project fell through when Hammerstein and Kern ended their partnership.

28. The policy was suspended for the duration of the production but immediately reinstated when the production ended.

29. Stark Young, review in *The New Republic*, 1935; cited in Hollis Alpert, *The Life and Times of* Porgy and Bess: *The Story of an American Classic* (New York: Alfred A. Knopf, 1990), 118.

a consensus that Gershwin had never made up his mind about what he was doing, and had produced a "folk opera" that was neither folkish and popular nor operatic and high-art, an unresolved mash-up rather than an achieved rendering of a definite concept. Virgil Thomson blasted Gershwin's work as "crooked folklore and halfway opera . . . a piquant but highly unsavory stirring-up-together of Israel, Africa, and the Gaelic Isles."[30] The critical opinion that the new work was, like Gullah English, halfway to something, and the fact that Gershwin cut and altered freely between early productions has allowed some directors to feel that they are effectively authorized by the author to change the work in ways that make it more coherent, complimentary to its subjects, or congenial to contemporary audiences. Since several of Gershwin's harsher critics, including Thomson, revised their estimates upward over time, there seems to be some uncertainty even among those who accuse Gershwin of uncertainty. Still, an inescapable conclusion from a survey of the history of critical debate surrounding *Porgy and Bess* is that a great many people, including performers and those who refused to perform, are troubled by the sense that there is something very wrong with it, that it is a perhaps magnificent realization of a muddled idea, that its greatness harbors a mysterious principle of self-betrayal, and that it would have benefited from more attention from Gershwin, whose tragic death in 1937 prevented him from giving his masterpiece the loving care it so richly deserved and so badly needed.

The all but visible appearance in critical discussions of Gershwin's "folk opera" of something like a hyphen, and the recurrence in these discussions of concepts of incompletion and incoherence, might suggest that Gershwin had found a way to create, *avant la lettre*, an operatic illustration of Walzer's America. But

30. Virgil Thomson, "George Gershwin," *Modern Music*, 13 (November–December 1935): 13, 16–17.

Gershwin was attempting to render the American experience without parentheses, and the flaws or blunders that some detect in his work are better understood as indicators of a different idea. Gershwin knew he had created a hybrid work that synthesized materials from different cultures, genres, and traditions, a work that sounded like nothing else, and that constituted a "new form" that had, he said, "come quite naturally out of the material."[31] The content of this new form, the "material" in question, and the source of the controversies, is the black people depicted in the opera. And here we come to the friction point, the source of most of the controversies surrounding the opera: the possibility that Gershwin was not merely confused or irresolute but insensitive and unwittingly complicit in assumptions of white supremacy and white privilege. This charge has never been uncontested and has never disappeared. Nor should it, for the eternal return of the issues of white supremacy and privilege lead us into the heart of the work itself.

A swirl of apparently conflicting charges circles fiercely around the issue of race. Some of the work's many critics have argued that Catfish Row is a "gentrified" or "unrealistic" version of black life, apparently on the premise that even opera is obliged to respect canons of realism and avoid stereotypes. (*Most barbers in Seville were honest tradesmen!*) Others who feel that works of art cannot be indifferent to considerations of social justice have claimed that Catfish Row is all too realistic, and fails to communicate the necessary point that black Americans

31. George Gershwin, "Rhapsody in Catfish Row: Mr. Gershwin Tells the Origin and Scheme for His Music in That New Folk Opera Called 'Porgy and Bess,'" *New York Times*, October 20, 1935, sect. 10: 1–2. Aware that he was creating a hybrid form, Gershwin nevertheless insisted that hybridity had its own character. In the same article, he is quoted as saying that while he tried to make his recitatives "as close to the Negro inflection in speech as possible," he had decided against using "original folk material because I wanted the music to be all of one piece."

are intelligent, capable, and hardworking, fully prepared to assume civic responsibilities in a democratic society.[32] Others have said that the characters as drawn by Heyward and Gershwin lack inner life, agency, or self-awareness.[33] Some have complained about what might be called the belief structure of Catfish Row, a heterodox but functional agglomeration of theology, magic, and superstition. A great many critics and even some performers have complained about the use of dialect—dialect written by the Nordic Heyward and the Jew Ira Gershwin, in a staging directed by the Georgian-Armenian Rouben Mamoulian—as a neo-minstrel affectation. Dialect had been an issue in the African American community since the turn of the century, when, as part of the effort to mount some resistance to what Henry Louis Gates describes as a "tidal wave of antiblack racism," "black dialect was scrubbed from the voices of black leaders"; Booker T. Washington and Du Bois sounded, as Gates notes, "for all intents and purposes, like Victorian white men" (*Stony the Road*, 200). *Porgy and Bess* brought this issue suddenly back into focus, and over the years some performers have on their own authority corrected their characters' speech, not just by refusing to sing the word nigger but also by standardizing pronunciations.

32. Hope Clark, directing a 1995 production by the Houston Grand Opera Company, claimed to be presenting authenticity and fact rather than stereotype. According to her "Coming from a black perspective, I know how we think, how we feel, what we do." Clark, who grew up in Washington, DC, and acted in *West Side Story* as a teenager before beginning a career dancing with the Katherine Dunham and Alvin Ailey companies, insisted that in reality the fictional characters on Catfish Row were "hard-working people . . . not slovenly, sit-around-all-day black people . . . they're upwardly mobile." Quoted in Valerie Scher, "Sportin' a New 'Porgy,'" *San Diego Union-Tribune*, March 5, 1995, D2, D8–9.

33. This charge is contested by Geoffrey O'Brien, who writes, "What is striking about *Porgy and Bess* in performance is how much freedom Gershwin's music allows for the exploration of character." O'Brien, "Back on Catfish Row," *New York Review of Books* November 21, 2019, 21.

In 1952 William Warfield sang about having "plenty of nothing," and Sammy Davis, Jr. occasionally spoke of his experience playing "Sporting Life" in the 1959 film.[34]

Behind all these varied and conflicting complaints is the suggestion that whatever the flaw in *Porgy and Bess* may be, that flaw arises from the fact that the whole thing is in the end only a white man's version of black life.

The revealing signature of the white man is an inability, despite one's best intentions—assuming they were the best—to depict black people without distortions resulting from bias or incomprehension, resulting in a parade of what are variously described as "degrading," "offensive," or "damaging" stereotypes, or in a phrase often attributed to Duke Ellington, "lampblack Negroisms."[35] From the very first—indeed, even in the play *Porgy* written by Heyward and (primarily by) his wife Dorothy that

34. See Sammy Davis at https://www.youtube.com/watch?v=acJBvqwuAIU. In *Ira Gershwin: The Art of the Lyricist,* Philip Furia argues that Gershwin and Heyward "came as close as any lyricists, white or black, to using that dialect as a medium of dignified and passionate expression" (113). Furia traces the use of dialect in songwriting to nineteenth-century minstrel shows, with limited use by black songwriters. The poetry of the Harlem Renaissance renounced dialect on principle, and so, Furia argues, it fell to Oscar Hammerstein to "forge that dialect into an instrument of powerful expressiveness." Then, in *Porgy and Bess*, Heyward and Ira Gershwin "achieved the greatest fulfillment of James Weldon Johnson's hope that a dialect so long used for racial caricature might become a medium for the full range of poetic expression" (115, 117–18).

35. While Ellington was accurately quoted as saying that Gershwin's music "was not distinctly or definitely negroid in character," the phrase "lamp-black Negroisms" is the interviewer's. While the comment is often taken as a judgment on *Porgy*'s portrayal of black people generally, in fact Ellington's criticism seems to center on just one song, "It Ain't Necessarily So." and may have been a response to the song's impiety, which Ellington found implausible. Edward Morrow, "Duke Ellington on Gershwin's 'Porgy,'" *New Theatre* 2 (December 1935): 6.

preceded by eight years Gershwin's opera—some cast members have been reluctant to appear to endorse by their performance depictions of a semi-literate, intemperate, disorderly, ill-informed, and politically docile black community. Some detected the possibility that the representations of black life might be used to justify the white monopoly on power, and protested in particular the use of the word nigger—which, however, remained in the libretto until 1952, when Ira Gershwin removed the last instance. (In writing the libretto, Heyward sometimes replaced the word used in the novel and the play by "nothin'," so that Serena tells Sportin' Life, "I can't remember ever meetin' a nothin' what I likes less than I does you."[36] But, for some, the insult remained even when the word was removed.

The word remained as long as it did in part because not everyone agreed that the modernizing alterations were improvements.

36. In the 1959 film directed by Otto Preminger, she says, "I can't remember ever meetin' a . . . [shrug] what I likes less than I does you." This film, almost universally considered a failure, was for many years difficult to find because Goldwyn destroyed most of the copies and the Gershwin estate repeatedly refused to grant permission for the film to be shown. A 2017 article asserted that only three prints were known to exist—one in the Library of Congress, another in the National Audiovisual Institute in Finland, and a third at The Clip Joint for Film in Burbank, CA. See Kim Masters, "David Geffen, Samuel Goldwyn, and the Search for the 'Holy Grail' of Missing Movies," *Hollywood Reporter* February 23, 2017, https://www.hollywoodreporter.com/features/david-geffen-samuel-goldwyn-search-holy-grail-missing-movies-977567. In 2020 the entire film was uploaded to YouTube: https://www.youtube.com/watch?v=YIdrZxaP-gE. The film eliminates the opera's recitative, substituting not Gullah speech but something that might be described as "standard English." For a discussion of the filming, see Pollack, *George Gershwin*, 648–54. See also Sharon Willis, *The Poitier Effect: Racial Melodrama and Fantasies of Reconciliation* (Minneapolis: University of Minnesota Press, 2015). Willis characterizes Poitier's most famous roles as that of a "magical Negro," and includes a chapter on "The Obsessive Sameness of Sidney Poitier."

Eva Jessye, who directed the chorus in three early productions including the first, regretted the bleaching of Bess's demand to Sportin' Life that he pocket his happy dust when "Take dat stuff away, nigger!" became "Take dat stuff away, Buzzard!" because it removed the line's "gut-bucket quality."[37] Dorothy Heyward pointed out in her defense that the word was used "fifty times a day" in the black community in Charleston. But critics argued that that was no defense because the complaint was not that the use of the word was unrealistic but that it had been written by white people for black people to speak, against their own interests.[38] In the late 1950s, it was difficult to find actors to star in Samuel Goldwyn's film of the opera; Sidney Poitier, who was then at the beginning of a period in which he would portray a series of "mainstream" images of black people (*The Defiant Ones* [1958], *All the Young Men* [1960], *Lilies of the Field* [1963], *Guess Who's Coming to Dinner* [1967], and *In the Heat of the Night* [1967]), thought the role demeaning and agreed to participate only to avoid jeopardizing his chances to get future roles.

The phrase "white man's vision of Negro life," occurs in one of the most widely cited responses to the film, James Baldwin's 1959 essay, "On Catfish Row: *Porgy and Bess* in the Movies."[39] Bluntly calling the film a disaster, Baldwin criticizes virtually everything about it, even Poitier's Porgy and Dorothy Dandridge's Bess. But he reserves his harshest criticism for those responsible for the film, including Heyward, Gershwin, and above all the Jewish, Ukrainian-born director Otto Preminger, a spectacularly bad choice, Baldwin says, "to direct a Negro cast" (617). Because of his background, and because "black people still do

37. Eva Jessye, quoted in Pollack, *George Gershwin*, 611.

38. Dorothy Heyward, quoted in Alpert, *Life and Times*, 59.

39. James Baldwin, "On Catfish Row: *Porgy and Bess* in the Movies" (1959), in Toni Morrison, ed., *James Baldwin: Collected Essays* (New York: Library of America, 1998), 618. All references to Baldwin's works are from this volume.

not, by and large, tell white people the truth," Preminger could only manage to tell the story of Catfish Row as a fantasy—in fact, as "the cruelest fantasy of all," that black life is "a better life—better in the sense of being more honest, more open, and more free: in a word, more sexual" (617, 619). Whites find this fantasy not just exciting but useful, Baldwin says, because it justifies keeping black people—whose existence, as Thomas Jefferson had noted, "appears to participate more of sensation than reflection"—in Catfish Rows all over the country, where they can lead their squalid, pullulating lives out of sight if not out of mind. Confined within the circumference of white ignorance, prejudice, and envy, the film "assuages [white people's] guilt about Negroes and it attacks none of their fantasies" (619). Baldwin may have been thinking not just of the film but of the production sponsored by State Department that toured Europe and Russia in 1952, and was promoted as evidence of the American commitment to freedom, justice, interracial harmony, and artistic expression at a time when black people could not, in many places, stay in hotels, eat at restaurants, or vote.[40]

Baldwin's oeuvre contains many indictments of the seemingly infinite white capacity for fantasy, and of the "incredible, abysmal, and really cowardly obtuseness of white liberals" in particular.[41] And he is correct in identifying in Heyward's *Porgy* an explicitly stated authorial envy for the rich sensuality and

40. The Moscow performance of this cacophonous production, which originally starred William Warfield, Leontyne Price, Cab Calloway, and Maya Angelou, was attended by Bulganin, Molotov, and Khrushchev. See *Porgy and Bess* CD, recorded live at Titiana Palast, Berlin. 1952, Kritzerland, 2018. The following year Senator Joseph McCarthy denounced Gershwin's music as "subversive." "'Gershwin's Music Subversive' Says Senator McCarthy," *Melody Maker* (13 June 1953); cited in Pollack, *George Gershwin*, 209.

41. James Baldwin, "Down at the Cross," in *The Fire Next Time* (1963), 320.

solidarity of Gullah culture that was soon to be sacrificed, Heyward sensed, on the altar of modernity. But it is hard to identify the reality that Baldwin feels is distorted by white obtuseness. The image of the psychic life of black people that emerges from Baldwin's work, both fiction and nonfiction, is strikingly bleak—complex, secretive, hunted, tragic, unrealized, with rare opportunities for expression, little capacity for agency, and virtually no interest in sharing intimacies with, or even speaking honestly to, white people. Baldwin repeatedly invokes a Negro essence that is inaccessible to white people both because whites do not make the effort and because blacks conceal themselves.[42] He describes "Black English" as a language incomprehensible to white people, a language in fact created so that black people could speak to one another freely in the presence of whites.[43] Clearly, Baldwin

42. As Baldwin said elsewhere, "It is a question, after all, whether what we will here call the ordinary American of good will knows anything more about Negro life than what has filtered through to him via memories of an exemplary Negro maid, or the experience—for which he is almost certainly not prepared—of, say, some Billie Holiday records. . . ." Baldwin, "The Crusade of Indignation," 610. For an account of black responses to *Porgy and Bess*, see Ray Allen and George P. Cunningham, "Cultural Uplift and Double Consciousness: African American Responses to the 1935 Opera *Porgy and Bess*," *The Musical Quarterly* 88 (Fall 2005) 3: 342–369. See also Ellen Noonan, *The Strange Career of* Porgy and Bess*: Race, Culture, and America's Most Famous Opera* (Chapel Hill: University of North Carolina Press, 2012), 143–49; Ibid. 173–83. It is worth noting that Gershwin's first Porgy, Todd Duncan, wrote that Heyward and Gershwin "had put down on paper accurately and truthfully something from the depth of soul of a South Carolina Negro woman." Duncan quoted in Merle Armitage, ed., *George Gershwin* (London: Longmans, Green, 1938), 60.

43. James Baldwin, "If Black English Isn't a Language, Then Tell Me, What Is?" (1979), 780–83. The idea of a single black identity to which white people have no access was put to the test by the original 1935 production of the opera. According to the Russian-born coach of the singers, the New York singers, some of them classically trained, who tried out for the cast often "hadn't the slightest trace of the essential Negro lingo" and

wanted to claim a deep and consistent black difference, but on several occasions he insisted that black people were "just like everybody else," that not only is black life no "better" than white life, it is no different (619).[44] It almost appears to be the case that, for Baldwin, any characterization of blacks by whites must be a mischaracterization.

Baldwin raises a question whose implications reach deep into American history and culture: Given the nation's history of denying the right of political representation to black people, by what right do white people undertake to represent black people in any way at all? This is the question, with its attendant political, moral, social, and artistic implications, that has haunted *Porgy and Bess* from the very beginning.

As Baldwin acknowledges, the beginning of the beginning is Heyward's novel, and so this question should in the first instance be put not to *Porgy and Bess* but to *Porgy*. In a startling moment, Baldwin exempts Heyward from his general charge of white ignorance, saying that the novelist "loved the people he was writing about" (618). Baldwin does not say that Heyward wrote from the inside of Gullah culture. One loves from the outside, and *Porgy* is conceived and narrated by one who lives

---

had to learn it through instruction. Alexander Steinert, cited in James M. Hutchisson, *DuBose Heyward: A Charleston Gentleman and the World of* Porgy and Bess (Jackson: University Press of Mississippi, 2000), 154. During rehearsals Todd Duncan, who played Porgy, told Gershwin that the composer was "more Negro than the actor was. Gershwin, in turn, joked that Duncan was more Jewish than Gershwin himself." Cited in Hutchisson, *DuBose Heyward*, 155. According to Horowitz, the Armenian-born director Rouben Mamoulian had the same problem with the cast of the play *Porgy* and hired a South Carolina expert on Gullah culture to coach them. And although English was his seventh language, Mamoulian had to "work in detail on almost every single word" with cast members (Horowitz, 35).

44. See also James Baldwin, "The American Dream and the American Negro" (1965), 717–18.

near, but not in, Catfish Row. This was Heyward's situation. Following the sudden death of his father, his mother eked out a living as a "dialect recitalist" telling Gullah stories to audiences, eventually becoming well known, even famous, in the region. Her son learned the dialect and the sensibility behind it as well as anyone not Gullah could. Indeed, his biographer speculates that Gullah might have been his first language (Hutchisson, *DuBose Heyward*, xviii). With the possible exception of Sportin' Life, who seems both an updated version of the minstrel figure of the "zip coon" and the serpent in the garden of Golden-Age Catfish Row, Heyward's characters, especially Porgy and Bess, are sharply individuated and capable of a wide range of moods and responses. They aspire, suffer, fear, love, dream, lust, despair, hate, fight, surrender, worship, and generally make their way through life. Bess reflects bitterly and realistically on her weaknesses, and Porgy on the existential isolation of the cripple; both undergo great and plausible changes in response to changing circumstances. As Baldwin seems to have understood, they represent the most fully developed black characters to appear in American fiction to that time.[45]

Neither Heyward nor his narrator—who occasionally speaks in the first person—pretends to be other than a white man. A descendant of a signer of the Declaration, Heyward was never in doubt about the gulf that separated him from the people he wrote about. No citizen of Catfish Row would describe someone

45. This was certainly Heyward's ambition. As he wrote to a dissertation student in 1933, he had grown to see "the primitive Negro as neither a professional comedian, nor an object for sentimental charity, but a racially self-conscious human being, living out his destiny beside us, and guided by a code." Letter, quoted in Nannie Elizabeth Creighton, *DuBose Heyward and His Contribution to Literature*, Master's Thesis, University of South Carolina, 1933, 24. As Hutchisson says, *Porgy* "could arguably be said to be the first psychologically true depiction of an African American by a white southerner" (*DuBose Heyward*, 63).

as "black with the almost purple blackness of unadulterated Congo blood," dozing "as only a full-blooded negro can"; no Negro would note "the odd fusion of comedy and tragedy so inextricably a part of negro life in its deep moments," nor would any churchgoing woman such as Serena note the risible oddity of the mishmash of Gullah beliefs and spiritual practices (*Porgy*, 17, 18, 29). Nor, for that matter, would any such citizen, limited by poverty, lack of knowledge, and the many burdens of a hard and uncertain life, have the emotional leisure to reflect that they were all living in a Golden Age. Nor would any feel that their culture—a term and concept few would understand—was especially admirable, or interesting, or precious, or anything at all other than life as it was lived. No Catfish Row resident would describe the parade of the Sons and Daughters of Repent Ye Saith the Lord as having "taken the reticent, old Anglo-Saxon town and stamped their mood swiftly and indelibly into its heart" (95). Without being radical or even progressive—although he became more so with time—Heyward was deeply knowledgeable and sympathetic and wrote in an elegiac tone about a people ill prepared for the urban life that circumstance had forced on them, and about a way of life that was vanishing before his eyes. Heyward's work, and its transmogrification by Gershwin, constitute not just the most eloquent or "loving," but almost the only memorial of that community at that time. Reviewing the novel, W. E. B. Du Bois described it as "a beautiful piece of work," and invaluable as a portrait of a culture that would otherwise be gone, gone, gone. *Porgy* is, Du Bois said, "the best, almost the only picture" of Gullah life in Charleston.[46]

46. W. E. B. Du Bois, "'Porgy,' by DuBose Heyward" (1926), in Nathan Huggins, ed., *W. E. B. Du Bois Writings* (New York: Library of America, 1986), 1215. Heyward's views, which seem regressive today, were always advanced, or at least idiosyncratic, in the context of white Charleston, and became more progressive as he spent time in New York, beginning in 1927 when he staged the play of *Porgy*. Heyward met, and was admired by, many

Neither Heyward nor Gershwin believed that ignorance implied stupidity, that unfamiliarity with the larger world signified smallness of mind or soul, that poverty was incompatible with dignity, or that dialect was inferior to standard English. Neither held the view that Baldwin attributed to white artists in general, that "whiteness is a kind of salvation and that blackness is a kind of death."[47] Indeed, in *Porgy and Bess,* all black people sing, often communally in massive choric utterances, while the few white characters speak, individually and unpleasantly. Neither Heyward nor Gershwin believed that a white man's version of black life was necessarily delusional and prejudicial, or that black people were unknowable. Their work suggests, rather, a conviction that the attempt to understand was an imperative placed on the present by history. They did not believe that black people were so profoundly immiserated that they were incomprehensible to others, that the circle of human empathy could never expand wide enough to take them in, or that they were doomed to be utter strangers to anyone outside their small and embattled

---

of the leading figures of the Harlem Renaissance, including James Weldon Johnson, Langston Hughes, Jean Toomer, Zora Neale Hurston, Alain Locke, and Nella Larsen. By depicting black people in sober and realistic (non-vaudevillian) terms, and by insisting that all black characters be played by black actors, Heyward and his wife overturned longstanding practice and significantly advanced the black theater movement in New York. In 1929 Heyward published a second and more ambitious novel about Gullah characters, *Mamba's Daughters*, which marks a far more critical and progressive position and includes satirical portraits of white Charleston society. By this time Heyward had become firmly linked with the issue of race relations, having joined the advisory board of the Association of Negro Writers and the Writer's League against Lynching. Several of Heyward's essays touching on the representation of black people in art are included in *A DuBose Heyward Reader*, ed., James M. Hutchisson (Athens: University of Georgia Press, 2003). The most important is the earliest, published in 1923, "And Once Again—the Negro," 13–16.

47. James Baldwin, "The Image of the Negro" (1948), 584.

group. On the evidence of their work, Heyward and Gershwin believed in the possibility of an honest representation and would have defended their own right as artists to make the effort.[48]

This right to represent actually takes human form in the works themselves in the form of Alan Archdale, a lawyer who helps to release Old Peter, who had been jailed as a "material witness" in the murder of Crown. In Heyward's *Porgy*, Archdale says he represents a family that "must have owned half the slaves in the county," adding that now, "I look after their colored folks for them" (53). Archdale treats black people, who regard the legal profession as a mysterious meshwork of threats to be given as wide a berth as possible, with an uncondescending familiarity, good humor, and even affection that is still never mistaken for a relation between social equals. He sees to it that the charlatan "divorce" lawyer Frazier is not put out of business, understanding that while the documents he sells have no legal status (divorce being illegal in South Carolina at that time), Frazier provides a service considered valuable in the community. Mediating between white and black communities, Archdale embodies the possibility of good-faith representation that observes the customs of both. Like Velázquez in "Las Meninas," Heyward has included in his work an image of himself, the white man creating the version in which otherwise unrepresented black people come to countenance in a form that does them some justice.

Nor is Archdale the only white presence in Catfish Row. Baldwin complains that "what has always been missing from George Gershwin's opera is what the situation of Porgy and Bess says about the white world" (adding that this omission is the reason "Americans are so proud of the opera") (618–19). But

48. Gershwin's right to represent black people would in all likelihood also have been defended by Todd Duncan, who told Ned Rorem that when he first heard Gershwin play the music on the piano, "I literally wept for what this Jew was able to express for the Negro." Ned Rorem, "Living with Gershwin," *Opera News* (March 16, 1985): 16.

while white characters appear only occasionally in Gershwin's opera, their influence is ubiquitous, a fact more easily seen in Heyward's novel, with its more detailed portrayal of the interactions between the races. When a crime occurs on Catfish Row, white police come to investigate. Understanding that no Gullah will turn one of their own over to the police even for an act of murder, they imprison Peter in an act that seems capricious, cruel, and unjust, but that gives people the only incentive they have to free him by naming the murderer. (Peter is still imprisoned, for a week, as a "material witness.") If a black person is thrown in prison (as one might be, the narrator notes, "if one added to the handicap of a dark skin the indiscretion of swallowing cocaine and indulging in a crap game"), the jailors were "not vindictive. They were not even unkind. Some of them evidenced a mild affection for their charges and would pause to exchange greetings with them on their rounds" (78–79). But the influence of white culture on Catfish Row is not limited to the justice system. Porgy is supported by white ("Buckra") charity. When Bess falls ill, Peter says "One ob my w'ite folks is er nuss tuh de hospital; and dat lady is er pur angel wid de sick nigger" (83).[49] If a black corpse threatens to rot, white officials step in and threaten to take the corpse and "give um tuh de students," serving the cause of health care in the city (28). The legal system, the police, the medical profession, and various individuals all have the power and, it seems, a sense of responsibility to reach into the community to do what needs to be done, the resistance to such intrusions notwithstanding. Without such reach, beggars would starve, crime would go unpunished, people would languish (even

49. Peter continues his praise by saying that if he fell ill, he would go to the hospital to be cared for by this woman because "I wants dis carcase tek care ob w'ile he is alive. Wen he done dead, I ain't keer." Challenged as to whether he is really willing to be "cut up an' scatter, 'stead of bein' bury in Gawd own grabe-yahd," Peter says, "Well, mebbe I ain't sayin I jus' as lief . . . but I t'ink Gawd onduhstan' de succumstance, an' mek allowance" (83).

longer) in jail, illness would go untreated, corpses would rot, and medical knowledge would not advance. Of course, boundaries must be observed. When Sportin' Life comments on the attractiveness of the white women in Charleston, Maria sets him right, telling him that "Dis county ain't nebber yit see a black man git lynch. Dese nigger knows folks, an' dey knows nigger. Fer Gawd' sake keep yuh mout' off w'ite lady" (50–51). All this is if not directly represented at least alluded to in *Porgy and Bess.*

To live on Heyward's Catfish Row is, then, not to live in a pristine organic Gullah community; it is to live in a "white man's version," surrounded and encumbered, but also, in sometimes unfeeling and unpredictable ways, to be cared for and even valued by what Walzer had referred to as a "rational-legal authority" that ensures that the black community will have the protections of a law it neither comprehends nor respects (other than as power), without having to forget who or what they are. It is to be subjected to, but also occasionally represented by forces in which one has no share. The two communities are bound by a principle of partial intelligibility. Heyward's white characters can communicate with the black characters, understanding their speech if not always their motivations, and appreciating facts if not always values. And Heyward's highly literary and ironic narrator presents the unbleached and grammatically nonstandard speech of his characters to the reader in the confidence that both his discourse and theirs can be understood as variants on a common tongue.

This elementary formal feature of narrative has, in the case of *Porgy and Bess,* more than formal implications. One of the enabling fictions of fiction is that characters have a certain independence from the narrator who creates them but who, in writing dialogue, records rather than invents. It is part of this pretense that in setting down the speech of his characters, the author cedes some control of his work to his creations. If the characters do not persuasively speak for and as themselves, they may come to seem mere emanations of the narrator's mind, and the entirety risks being understood as a monologue, with the narrator imagining rather than witnessing and reporting, dreaming or hallucinating rather than documenting events in the world. If, on the other hand, the characters establish so much autonomy that the narrative voice is reduced to reportage, the entirety threatens to become a melee, a centerless assemblage of utterances lacking the direction or structure that an encompassing narration could provide. The artistic success of the narrative hangs on a complicated nesting of pretenses within pretenses: the author must appear to believe in, solicit, and honor the freedom and in a sense the equality of his characters, who for their part must exercise that freedom only within the bounds established by the author.

One of the most commonly voiced experiences connected to the creative process is that at some point the work itself takes over and directs its own emergence. So intensely has the author imagined the characters that she becomes creatively confused about what is real and what is not. The novelist Hilary Mantel, to take a single recent example, has described the experience of creation as one of persuading herself that she is not creating, but merely listening. "There's a point where you're living with these people and only with them," she says; "they're more real and solid to you than actual people in your life."[50] The experience is often reported to be liberating. Creation can be a daunting task, but, when can-do characters take over the heavy lifting, the author can experience a sudden confidence in her ability to execute the more modest reportorial or stenographic tasks of observation

50. Quoted by Alexandra Alter, "For Hillary Mantel, There's No Time like the Past," *New York Times*, 24 February 2020, https://www.nytimes.com/2020/02/24/books/hilary-mantel-mirror-and-the-light-thomas-cromwell.html. For a well-traveled and often-reprinted anthology of accounts of the creative process, see Brewster Ghiselin, ed., *The Creative Process: A Symposium* (Berkeley: University of California Press, 1952).

and transcription. Versions of this fiction can be found in the accounts of composers, painters, sculptors, and choreographers, but writers seem to experience a particularly compelling form of it because their work involves human beings who speak and act—and maybe even write—just as the author does. Heyward had the advantage of having read about "a beggar named Smalls" in the newspaper, so he did not have to invent a human being and then try to persuade himself he had not done so, but he understood the dynamics of the creative process, and described his Porgy as a white man's version of a real person, "a creature of my imagination . . . upon whom, being my creation, I could impose my own . . . conception."[51]

Belief in imaginary friends can have political implications. As Edmund S. Morgan has pointed out, any government founded on some idea of "the people" lodges this make-believe in the heart of governance. "Before we ascribe sovereignty to the people," he writes, "we have to imagine that there is such a thing."[52] The English undertook this thought experiment in the seventeenth century and the Americans in the late eighteenth, when, in the Declaration and then in the Constitution, "the people" were "invented," that is, declared to exist and to be capable of intentionality and purposive action. A further entanglement of government and the writing of fiction was created by the institution of "representation" as the means by which the people would exercise the power that political philosophy had granted them. "Representation," Morgan says, "is itself a fiction" in that

51. DuBose Heyward, quoted in Dorothy Heyward, "Foreword," DuBose Heyward, *Porgy*, 11–12. In the midst of the writing process, Heyward wrote to his friend Hervey Allen that "the Spirit of God has been perched on the studio gable for a month, and where the stuff came from else, I can't imagine." Letter of 15 July 1924, quoted in Hutchisson, *Dubose Heyward*, 54.

52. Edmund S. Morgan, *Inventing the People: The Rise of Popular Sovereignty in England and America* (New York: W. W. Norton, 1988), 153.

while the people are held to be the sole legitimate source of power, they are in fact compelled to submit to laws passed by their governors (23). This paradox of being subject to your own creation while still in some sense possessing all the power—the "central enigma of popular sovereignty," as Morgan says—mirrors the relation between the narrator, whose legitimacy and effectiveness are manifest in the persuasive autonomy of his creation, and the characters, whose autonomy is entirely an effect created by the narrator (39).

According to Ian Watt's classic study *The Rise of the Novel*, extended prose fiction and democratic sentiments not only came to prominence together over the course of the eighteenth century but reinforced each other.[53] To the factors of individualism, realism, and populism whose effects Watt traces, another could be added that had great pertinence especially in the American colonies, the provocative resemblance of the relation between the British Crown and the American colonies on the one hand and the fictional narrator and his characters on the other. The American Revolution could be described, and in a sense described itself, as the rebellion of people who felt that they were, to the king, mere fictions, simulacra whose reality was limited to the use he could make of them; and that among other "injuries and usurpations," they were being exploited (i.e., taxed) without proper representation. As fictional characters will and must, they

53. Ian Watt, *The Rise of the Novel: Studies in Defoe, Richardson, and Fielding* (Berkeley: University of California Press, 1957). The rise of the novel in America can be seen as one factor in the shift from a republican to a democratic society after the Revolution. As Cathy Davidson argued in *Revolution and the Word*, the vehement opposition to novel-reading by republican-aristocrats, including Thomas Jefferson, suggests that they sensed a dangerous connection between the forms of imaginative freedom cultivated by fiction and the chaos of democracy. Cathy Davidson, *Revolution and the Word: The Rise of the Novel in America* (New York: Oxford University Press, 1986).

declared an independence from the sovereign-narrator. In doing so, they asserted a liberty already implicitly granted them by a nation long celebrated for its devotion to individual freedom. The fact that the rebels were claiming a principle that the king himself recognized and honored put the king in a difficult position, unable to crush the rebellion without violating his own commitments. As Edmund Burke put it in a debate in Parliament in support of the colonial uprising, the American revolution was a thoroughly English undertaking, with the rebels "not only devoted to liberty, but to liberty according to English ideas, and on English principles."[54] If English soldiers were to take arms against the revolutionaries, they would, Burke argued, be opposing their own heritage. Burke lost the debate and the English the war, and the colonies obtained the right of self-representation. In effect, the rebels had exploited the convention of fiction that had initially trapped them in the fantasy of another person—a "white man"—to overthrow the established hierarchy.

By winning, however, the rebels had become "white men" themselves through their displacement or extermination of Indians, their silent denial of full civil rights to women, and their importation of hundreds of thousands of black people, who were now in the same position, narratively speaking, as their masters had been under the Crown. The revolution may have been, as one historian puts it, "in favor of government,"[55] but since the

54. Edmund Burke, "Speech on Conciliation with America," in Warren M. Elofson, John A. Woods, and William B. Todd, eds., *The Writings and Speeches of Edmund Burke, Volume 3: Party, Parliament, and the American War: 1774–1780* (Oxford, UK: Clarendon Press, 1996), 120.

55. Max M. Edling, *A Revolution in Favor of Government: Origins of the U.S. Constitution and the Making of the American State* (Oxford, UK: Oxford University Press, 2003). For the argument that the Revolution was motivated by the desire for a state that would actively promote prosperity and equality, see Steven Pincus, *The Heart of the Declaration: The Founders' Case for Activist Government* (New Haven, CT: Yale University Press, 2016).

government was founded on principles of liberty and equality, American society could not be anything other than dynamic, even incomplete and incoherent. As long as some kind of inequality in rights, access, protection, or opportunity existed, the case could be made that the nation was in conflict with itself, and that the white men of the nation were hoarding privileges that by right should be equally shared. This was the case made in 1852 by Frederick Douglass as he began his mighty peroration "The Meaning of July Fourth for the Negro" by recalling the sublimity of the occasion on July 4, 1776, and commanding his listeners—the citizens of Rochester in attendance at a celebration sponsored by the Rochester Ladies' Anti-Slavery Sewing Society—to "Cling to this day—cling to it," before denouncing the entire occasion as a sham because he, an escaped slave, could not share in their patriotic pride.[56] The prevailing sentiment among abolitionists at the time was that the fine phrases of the Declaration had been betrayed by the Constitution, which silently countenanced the continuation of slavery. Breaking with his friends and allies, Douglass argued in this talk that the Declaration was the foundation of freedom and the Constitution a "glorious liberty document," because it nowhere explicitly mentioned slave, slavery, or slaveholding (202). After the end of the Civil War, this ingenious and peculiar argument, which simply ignored the Constitution's euphemism of "persons bound to service," proved to be effective, and has been supported by the courts ever since. For Douglass, the white man's version in the nation's foundational documents was an indispensable weapon in the fight for freedom and equality.

The necessary inference from this interpretation of Douglass's argument is that in order for the work of freedom to

56. Frederick Douglass, "The Meaning of July Fourth for the Negro," in Philip S. Foner, ed., *Life and Writings of Frederick Douglass*, five vols., (New York: International Publishers, 1950–75), II, 185; Ibid. 192.

proceed, there must be white men—people of privilege, people who enjoy greater status or protections than others—who, in the course of their ascension, claimed and committed themselves publicly to principles of freedom and equality. The precondition of progress in a society committed to freedom and equality is the existence of a white man's version whose legitimacy can be contested because the contest is embedded in the version. Novels might, as Thomas Jefferson believed, lead to sloppy thinking and emotional turbulence especially in females, but this narrative *dérangement* serves the interests of those who, like Jefferson and other Americans before the Revolution, find themselves more narrated than narrating.[57] The invitation extended by narrators to their characters to assert autonomy makes for persuasive fiction; and when, like Heyward and then Gershwin, white authors create black characters who speak, or sing, for themselves, they set in motion a sequence that may begin with a wink and a nod but might end in the authors' own supercession.

This American drama of representation is the subject of Gershwin's opera, presented both in its content, through the figure of Archdale, and in its form as created by Heyward and Gershwin.

At the beginning of their American lives, all immigrant groups must contend with life in a white man's version of the world in which they feel themselves misunderstood and undervalued, and, worse, in which they are told that they must forget their origins and become "white" in order to become full citizens. Black people experience this challenge in a particularly

57. Jefferson denounced the "inordinate passion prevalent for novels" as a "great obstacle to good education." The result of excessive novel-reading was "a bloated imagination, sickly judgment, and disgust towards all the real businesses of life." Letter to N. Burwell, March 14, 1818, in H. A. Washington, ed., *The Writings of Thomas Jefferson*, vol. 7 (Washington, DC: Taylor and Maury, 1854), 102.

poignant way in that the nation had deliberately "forgotten" them in its founding documents and social practices, and because, even after Emancipation, they could never become literally white, their skin continuing to signify the presumed inferiority that had been used to explain their otherwise inexplicable and indefensible servitude in a nation committed to equality and freedom. But all groups possess some marker of difference or foreignness, some token of identity that may appear to be easily dispensed with, but which carries a great deal of meaning as the manifest of their origins, origins not chosen but given, and that cannot be forgotten without a loss of identity itself. Becoming American has for all groups entailed a denial or concealment of the proposition that one is who one is, not who one pretends or aspires to be. The controversies swirling around every new production of *Porgy and Bess* replay and reactivate this fundamental drama, and trauma, of American history.

The real characters of the opera, in this reading, are not Porgy, Bess, and the others, and not black people generally, but all those who come to America from elsewhere. The real setting is not Catfish Row but the world; New York is America. Black people occupy the stage, but they are not the essential focus; they are the water through which the wave of the larger drama passes. The white man's version of black life presented in the opera is not the distorted form of a black reality, but the content, the true subject of the opera.

This reading is based not on Heyward's novel alone but on the transformation of the novel effected by Dorothy Heyward, who, shortly after her marriage to DuBose, created, largely by herself, a version of *Porgy* for the stage. The play removes, of course, Heyward's narration, but also changes the plot by having Bess taken off not to Savannah by "fishmen" but to New York by Sportin' Life. Returning to Catfish Row after his release from prison, Porgy learns of Bess's departure; informed of the direction of New York, he "turns his goat and drives slowly, with bowed head, toward the gate," apparently intending to rescue her from Sportin' Life as he had rescued her from Crown.[58] Seemingly intended as a more hopeful ending than the total desolation of the novel, which ends with a crushed Porgy collapsed outside his door in "an irony of morning sunlight," this new conclusion takes the story out of Charleston and aligns it loosely with the Great Migration, in which hundreds of thousands of black people left their homes in the South for the opportunities available in the urban North, transforming the ethnography of the novel into sociology (158).[59] Then, in a final and decisive turn of the screw, Rouben Mamoulian, the play's director, added Porgy's line "Bring m' goat!," and the declaration, "I'm on my way," converting hopelessness into defiance and sociology into epic, and making of the story a fit subject for opera.[60]

Porgy's grandly delusional determination puts him in the same category as other American dreamers (including Jay Gatsby, who "wed his unutterable visions to [Daisy's] perishable breath"), but the implications of this micromigration are less than grand. The three characters who set out on the trek to New York obey different imperatives, none inspiring: Sportin' Life is a thoroughly criminalized, almost demonic figure who returns to Catfish Row and, after repeated efforts, succeeds in carrying off

58. Stage direction, Dorothy and DuBose Heyward, *Porgy* (Studio City, CA: Players Press, Inc., 2005), 83.

59. On the Great Migration, see Isabel Wilkerson, *The Warmth of Other Suns: The Epic Story of America's Great Migration* (New York: Vintage, 2010).

60. Stephen Sondheim has called "Bring my goat!" "one of the most moving moments in musical theater history." Sondheim quoted in *New York Times*, 10 August 2011; cited in Horowitz, *"On My Way,"* 1–2. The argument that Mamoulian decisively altered the character of the play *Porgy*, transforming it from "a quasi-realistic regional cameo into an epic theater work, a parable of suffering and redemption" that carried over to his staging of *Porgy and Bess*, is made by Horowitz on the basis of a discovery in the Mamoulian archive at the Library of Congress of two versions of the play's final script: a handwritten version with revisions in Mamoulian's hand and a final typescript that incorporated those revisions.

Bess, whose body will support him in his New York hotels; Bess is ensnared through desperation and weakness; and Porgy's ambitions are so manifestly doomed that the best one might hope for him is that he fails quickly and returns to Catfish Row, defeated but alive.[61] While the process of becoming-American can be described in glorious or mythic terms, *Porgy and Bess* focuses on the smaller disasters, visible only from close range, of a process that grinds up individuals in the mill of a larger collective aspiration. The lyrics of "There's a Boat Dat's Leavin' Soon for New York" ("that's where we belong, Sister!") declare a joyous desire to modernize and Americanize (like other immigrants who had arrived in New York by boat) but, in the mouth of Sportin' Life, also suggest the cost of that aspiration both for the individual and for the culture as a whole. As more and more citizens on Catfish Row heed the call and head North, eventually to become "African Americans," memories of Gullah culture will fade into the kind of Golden-Age dream Heyward documents.[62] This dream, the tragic recollection of a more enveloping

61. As Henry Louis Gates notes, "the arrival of their Southern brethren could be discomfiting to some of the New Negroes" already living in Harlem, many of whom had lived in the North for generations. One can imagine how Porgy, if he could somehow succeed in his quest, would fit into a group that "saw themselves as members of the black upper class, a cosmopolitan mobile elite that could be integrated into American society" (*Stony the Road*, 204).

62. Walzer suggests that black people took the name African American in emulation of the immigrant groups who had arrived long after them but who had been much more successful than they in acquiring rights (Walzer, 44–45, n. 30). It should be noted, however, that while W. E. B. Du Bois does not use the hyphenated form, he begins *The Souls of Black Folk* (1903) with a famous dilemma: "One ever feels his twoness,—an American, a Negro; two souls, two thoughts, two unreconciled strivings; two warring ideals in one dark body," a situation that results in a crippling "double consciousness." Later in the same essay, Du Bois speaks of the white presumption that black people were "half-men." W. E. B. Du Bois,

and sustaining way of life than the one currently inhabited, shadows the more celebrated American dream of assimilation, success, and individual freedom. As Catfish Rows are razed and replaced by affordable housing—or, in the actual case in Charleston, renovated to become expensive homes—the land becomes a double dreamscape, with the vanished culture lingering only as a monetized and fantasized never-was memory of itself.

Gershwin's conclusion suggests tragic outcomes for everyone, but by positing even these compromised forms of agency and transition, it also animates what would otherwise be a static image of black culture—the image presented in Heyward's novel—as a variegated but essentially unchanging scene of poverty, violence, worldly ignorance, and exclusion. Dynamism, change, and transformation may well be the ultimate themes of the work, which authorizes in advance the alterations to which it is subjected in each new production. "There can be no doubt," Geoffrey O'Brien writes, "that [Gershwin] intended not a work fixed unchangeably at a single point in time but a process of continuing change that would keep it vital" ("Back on Catfish Row," 21). The process is inexorable, and indifferent to the consequences. The three departures at the opera's ending may break the magic circle of the Gullah community, with its saucer-burials, parades, and island picnics, its intense group identification and loyalty, its communal child-rearing, but it also breaks a cycle of misery and exposure. Darkening the American dream in some ways, *Porgy and Bess* brightens it in others.

The pluralists Walzer describes might say that the lack of an organic American culture means that there are no distinctively American cultural forms, that nothing produced by a given community could possibly stand for the entirety. Gershwin would agree, in a sense, and would only propose a small modification,

"Of Our Spiritual Strivings," in *The Souls of Black Folk*, in *W. E. B. Du Bois Writings*, 364–65; Ibid., 369.

a slightly different pronunciation: nuttin', to which he ascribed a positive content. The nature of that content is indicated, albeit unintentionally, by Walzer who, in the course of arguing that Americanness is a composite of other cultures, suggests that American identity can still be expressed by "cultural artifacts of a quite specific sort." What kind? His example is "I Got Rhythm," which turned up in the 1951 film inspired by Gershwin's 1928 orchestral composition *An American in Paris,* when Gene Kelly tells French children he will show them "*une danse américaine.*" Walzer describes this song as an unsorted jumble of all the cultures abandoned by Americans when they came to the new country, a "melted-down combination of Northern English clog dancing, the Irish jig and reel, and African rhythmic foot stamping, to which had been added, by Kelly's time, the influence of the French and Russian ballet" (40). As noted earlier, the refrain of this song precisely anticipates "I Got Plenty o' Nuttin,'" which stands as the Gershwins'—George and Ira's—national anthem, a creative embrace of the circumstance of loss, despite its hardships and deprivations, that can stand comparison with other, older and more homogeneous cultures, and their dances.[63]

63. If "I Got Plenty o' Nuttin'" is the Gershwins's national anthem, with its allusions to enemies defeated, threats shrugged off, roads not taken—"I got no lock on de door, dat's no way to be"—then "I Got Rhythm," an unconflicted cry of exultation, is their "America the Beautiful." A "humble, ungrammatical pop song," as Will Friedwald puts it, "I Got Rhythm" is Gershwin's most widely heard piece of music. It established Gershwin's role as the key transitional figure between Irving Berlin and Jerome Kern (who wanted their music played exactly as written) and more jazz-oriented composers such as Hoagy Carmichael and Johnny Mercer (who encouraged the use of the melody as a point of departure for improvisations). "The whole movement of jazz from melodic improvisation to harmonic improvisation," Friedwald writes, "was largely made possible by 'Rhythm.'" Will Friedwald, *Stardust Melodies: A Biography of Twelve of America's Most Popular Songs* (New York: Pantheon Books, 2002), 190.

In Gershwin's view, America may be an anomaly—he may even have seen it as exceptional—but it is not anonymous. Its substantive identity is grounded not in traditions or language or geography but in the impulse to create something new out of the remnants of the old. This impulse begins with a nothing that is yet more than nothing: a kind of pulse or regularity detectable in oneself and in the world, a sense of rhythm that suggests the possibility of intentional form. In the introduction to the stage version of *Porgy,* Heyward speaks of rhythm as "the secret law" of black culture.[64] Through "I Got Rhythm" and "Fascinating Rhythm," the Gershwins extended the reach of rhythm; in the words of one writer, the brothers were "largely responsible for rhythm entering the vocabulary of millions of people for whom it had previously been too technical" a term.[65] One might suggest, in a generously Gershwinian spirit, that other cultures, insofar as they are creative, have access to the same secret law. Creation itself requires a deep attention to the possibilities for willed inflections and accentings of the regularities that govern life at all levels from the organic to the celestial, possibilities denied or obscured by static traditions or abstract concepts. Hillary Mantel describes recurrent dreams in which the words in a book disintegrate before her eyes—a terrifying experience of loss, except that "when you wake up, you've got the rhythm of a sentence in your head, but you don't know what the sentence was."[66] Beneath the words, beneath the meaning, and even beneath

64. DuBose Heyward, "Introduction," Dorothy Heyward and DuBose Heyward, *Porgy: A Play in Four Acts* (Garden City, NY: Doubleday, Doran, 1928), x.

65. William Austin, in conversation with Richard Crawford, cited in Richard Crawford, "George Gershwin's 'I Got Rhythm,'" Robert Wyatt and John Andrew Johnson, eds., *The George Gershwin Reader*, 157.

66. See Alexandra Alter, "For Hillary Mantel, There's No Time like the Past," *New York Times*, 24 February 2020, https://www.nytimes.com/2020/02/24/books/hilary-mantel-mirror-and-the-light-thomas-cromwell.html.

any intention, there is rhythm as pure possibility, the very ground and stuff of creation, a principle of implicit order that precedes and solicits invention, and serves, for Gershwin, as the core of American identity.[67]

Why, one might ask, would Gershwin try to tell this American story in the majestically alien form of opera, the least indigenous, even most un-American of all cultural forms? And then, why fill it with elements that deform opera itself, bending it in the direction of musical theatre? As we have seen, some Gershwin critics have explained the work's idiosyncrasies by suggesting that the composer never made up his mind which mode he wanted to work in. But Gershwin had meditated his work for years before he began to compose, and surely the stronger interpretation would be that he fully intended to create a hyphenated form, not because he saw America in these terms, as a collection of nationalities, but because he saw the world in these terms, with America taking its place among the others, one among many. Classical music, and opera in particular, is indigenous to no culture. Italians may disagree, but the ease with which the operatic form was adopted by other nations suggests that, in its extreme artifice, opera comes close to being a universal expressive form that is equally accessible, or perhaps equally foreign, to all. Entering the field of opera, *Porgy and Bess* declares that a new and distinctive American culture deserves to stand alongside the highest achievements of other nations. Just as Heyward's use of Gullah dialect had forced his readers to expand their sense of the parameters and possibilities of the English language, Gershwin's folk opera forces the stylized, conventional, and international form of opera to make way for the new rhythms of the *danse américaine.*

67. For Irving Berlin, the characteristic style of American music was the "new rhythm" created by "broken harmonies" and "ragged time." Berlin, quoted in Michael Freedland, *Irving Berlin* (New York: Stein & Day, 1974), 69.

CONCLUSION

A More Perfect Disunion

Working hard to get ready for the evening performance on the show boat, Pete—played by Arthur Hohl, a little-known film stalwart who would act in over one hundred films, specializing in villainous or mildly larcenous roles—is irritated that Queenie—played by Hattie McDaniel, the daughter of a former slave who would win an Oscar three years later for her role in *Gone with the Wind*—does not step aside to let him do his job. He vents. "Outta my way, 8-ball!" "Who wants to get in your way?" she replies, dismissing him a moment later with a hoot of laughter.

A quick little exchange occurring less than three minutes into *Show Boat*, this sequence triggers the entire plot. As she speaks, Pete notices she is wearing a brooch he had given to Julie LaVerne, the show boat's leading actress, as a token of his esteem. He realizes that his gift had not been received with the respect and gratitude he felt it deserved. Accusing Julie later of "giving my present to a colored cook," Pete receives no satisfaction, and is in fact beaten up by her husband Steve. His pride wounded, he avenges himself by telling the local authorities that Julie had a black mother and a white father, is consequently black, and that she and Steve are therefore a mixed-race couple whose marriage is illegal. As we have seen, complications ensue.

This confrontation is, however, important not just for its effects but for what it is in itself: a direct exchange between a white person and a black one. Pete sees someone in his way, she

"Outta my way, 8-ball."

sees someone who inspires no fear, and both say exactly what's on their minds.

So generally unworthy, unsympathetic, and uncouth is Pete —and so little authorial thought seems to have been devoted to his character—that there seems little to be gained from an attempt to probe his character, and no point at all in trying to depict him as a man of high ideals and liberal views. But the case can be made. To be sure, he had sought a romantic relationship with a married woman. But he had apparently been given reason to hope. He had gotten close enough to Julie for her to reveal a terrible secret known only to her husband. She had accepted the lovely token of his esteem that he had gallantly given (before passing it off to Queenie). His intentions and actions were as honorable as the dishonorable intentions and actions of a dishonorable man could be. He could be Sir Launcelot, except that instead of courting a queen, Pete was pursuing a woman he knew, or came to know, to be black and passing, and therefore not just dangerous to him but, if the truth were to become known, far lower (even) than he on the social scale.

In short, while Pete does not solicit middle-class admiration, he does not qualify as a "racist" and is, in the context of his time and place, actually progressive, a working-class avatar of courtship, romantic love, self-sacrifice, and an integrated world that was still far off in the future.

I trust that by now the reader will be in a state of open rebellion, for in that initial four-word directive, Pete had insulted Queenie—recognizable to audiences since 1939 and *Gone with the Wind* as a beloved and historically significant actress and a far greater star than Mr. Hohl would ever be—for her race, her looks, and her weight. It is hard to imagine a man doing greater damage to his standing in polite society with a single sentence. And yet Queenie does not seem to register the insult; or rather, she registers it but dismisses it, and departs triumphant: she had taunted and belittled him without cost—and she had kept the brooch. In a sense, Pete also got what he wanted: she moved away so he could do his job. No hard feelings, or at least no harder than they had been. Nor does Pete suffer any deferred consequences for his abusiveness. After telling the sheriff about Julie's parentage, he disappears, an unsavory but ultimately negligible figure who does not need to be punished in the film because the audience, like Queenie and Julie, no longer cares about him. In the film's management of this moment we can see a social world entirely different from the one inhabited by most Americans in the twenty-first century.

In many obvious respects, but especially with respect to racial issues, the world depicted in the first half of *Show Boat* is not one that people today would choose to live in, being hard, violent, punitive, racist, and unjust. It is the world of the past, and the prevailing view today is that great determination and vigilance are required to combat and overcome this past, lest we slide back into a default condition of unthinking bigotry. Today, race is not just a political, social, and historical issue, but a moral issue, connected to some of the starkest contrasts between good and evil, and some of the clearest moral causes, of recent times. Leaders in the struggle against racial discrimination and bigotry have long been accounted heroes worthy of the admiration and gratitude not just of black people but of the entire nation; indeed, a few even command international respect. Because of their efforts, great progress has been made both in law and in social behavior, even including ordinary speech. Depending on the context, someone who spoke today as Pete did might be publicly accused, immediately vilified, and soon unemployed or even unemployable.

Great progress has been made but nobody would claim that we are today living in the reign of love. By many measures, racial relations are at a painfully low ebb, with the safety, economic status, health, life expectancy, and social mobility of vast numbers of black people in particular remaining dismayingly low, even as voting rights are being restricted in many places. All of our vigilance, all of our determination to eradicate traces of past discrimination, have failed to advance the cause of justice or even to prevent regression, so that today racism is commonly described as "systemic" or "structural," that is, hard-wired or embedded, independent of the conscious intentions or wishes of individuals, and deeply resistant to modification. For many people today, the assertion of this analysis passes for incontrovertible common sense; for many others, the denial of this analysis is similarly self-evident. The general social discourse on race has become stalled, rigid, static, oppositional, accusatory, resistant, dug in.

The worlds represented in the three works that have centered this discussion are very different from one other, but they are even more different from the world of contemporary America. In none of them is the issue of race treated as a matter of overriding moral urgency. In fact, by contemporary standards, they seem at crucial moments to be cruelly indifferent to the concerns that have motivated their critics. To an extent that is today regarded as unacceptable, the characters represented in these works speak what they feel, not what they ought to say. But if the present can accuse the past, the past should be permitted at least to defend itself and even to make its case against the present. In this instance, the past might point out that the uncensored and unapologetic candor of Pete's initial statement represents an honest expression of his feelings, invites candor in return, and results in a live conversation between people who are, for the moment, equal in a limited but real way. Neither party seems to feel either burdened or empowered by history; neither feels that the exchange involves issues of immense importance; and neither feels that the claims of civility should trump those of frankness, which, they may say, is actually more indicative of the kind of respect for the other that anchors a society committed to the belief that all people are in crucial ways equal. Free speech, the foundation for so many other freedoms, is possible for Pete and Queenie even if a perfect social equality among all people is not. One can imagine a social order in which a certain amount of friction is tolerated as the cost of pursuing this more general equality. So, while such unprotected exchanges may seem —and be—insensitive to larger implications, inattentive to history, and full of the threat of backsliding, it is possible to think differently about them, and then, perhaps, differently about present needs.

All the works discussed here tolerate a great deal of friction; the question is whether they pursue in any way or to any degree the general equality on which America is founded and the more perfect union toward which America is said to strive. The answer I have given is that it is possible to see them in this light, not as one-dimensional monuments to a dishonorable past but as expressions of a culture groping its way, not always with a purposeful stride, not always with clear sight, and not always in good faith, toward a present moment that for all its imperfections is confident enough of its superiority to criticize them. The artistic flaws, moral shortcomings, and historical inaccuracies for which each work has been condemned might, in this reading, be seen as markers of a self-revealing unease, symptoms displayed by a work not fully harmonized with itself, a work reaching toward a more perfect artistic unity than it is able to achieve or even to imagine. Like America in Michael Walzer's account, these works are incoherent and incomplete. To the extent that they invite their own critique and even their own repudiation in the name of something better, we might consider their flaws as signs not of their failure but of their success in representing the self-criticizing, self-modifying, and sometimes self-improving spirit of the nation.

It is particularly significant in this context that each of these works depicts a world in flux, a world beyond the control of any one, or any one set of forces. This is the case even with *Birth of a Nation,* which, although it ends with an outsized figure of Christ, the "Gentle Prince," presiding with incongruous solemnity over a kind of May Day festival, with no "seed of disunion" in evidence (if one discounts the decidedly pagan and even bacchanalian character of the scene), speaks obsessively of racial mixing. Whether achieved through rape or romance, in the North or in the South, miscegenation commands constant attention in the film. Certain characters are horrified by it and others see it as a means to an end, but the thing itself proceeds, indifferent to the intentions or wishes of individuals, a biological process that makes use of individuals, whose little thoughts are simply irrelevant to the large facts of human desire and generation. Racial mixing as an instance and consequence of the underlying fact of human compatibility—the rock upon which the principle of human equality, and therefore America, is founded—could be considered the real, if altogether unintended and indeed explicitly repudiated, message of *Birth of a Nation.* As a narrative, the film focuses on individuals, and cannot actually depict this ultimate consequence, but by showing a peaceable all-white polis achieved by slaughter in the streets and sustained only by armed vigilance, the film reveals the instability and fragility of its own highly restricted form of "Liberty and union," and in this way implies the inevitable passing of the order it seems to celebrate.

Show Boat demonstrates a comparable awareness of the fragility of its own conclusion. The true origin of the plot, implied but not shown, is the rape of the slave woman that resulted in

Liberty and union

the birth of Julie. The fact that the daughter of a slave could make a successful (if precarious) life feigning whiteness, and that Magnolia could make a successful career feigning blackness argues for a common humanity that underlies and undermines all social arrangements based on the strict division of the races. This bedrock human equality in turn argues for a response to difference that does not deny or seek to obliterate it but learns from it. In the final whiplash scenes—the utter triumph of whiteness in a veritable meteor shower of wealth, family, self-approval, and public acclaim, followed immediately by a scene of the Mississippi River with Joe, or at least Joe's voice, singing about its endless rolling, a poignant reminder of the unchanged condition of black people—we see once again the instability, not to mention the morally disturbing inequity, of a social order in which some people profit from others who profit not at all. Like *Birth of a Nation, Show Boat* shows more than it knows, or seems to know. Arguing against their own celebratory and forgiving attitude towards the small group of people on whom the narrative concentrates its attention, both films point beyond themselves to a further reckoning.

The characters depicted in *Porgy and Bess* seem to be immured in their circumstances, frozen in poverty and culturally isolated on Catfish Row. But the novel depicting them integrated

Catfish Row into a larger frame of reference and represented it to a wider culture; and then Gershwin's transformation of that novel into opera integrated that integration into a transnational cultural form in which it could reach international audiences for years to come. Gershwin, like Heyward, believed in the possibility of a good-faith representation that would entertain and enrich an audience without falsifying or degrading its object. Such representations disclose and exploit points of permeability and potentiality in the many kinds of barriers separating a white culture content to retain its privileges from a black culture that that was not (yet) organized in protest and that did not (yet) aspire beyond itself. The Gullah culture of Charleston, South Carolina, in the first years of the twentieth century may have been destitute and politically inert, but the representation of that culture created by Heyward and recreated by Gershwin anticipated and even perhaps facilitated or contributed to other changes, beginning with the appearance of black singers and actors—some of whom may have begun their lives on some Catfish Row or other—on a Broadway stage.

None of these works can be called unequivocally progressive in its politics. But progress can proceed on many paths. Art in general enlarges and populates the imagination by offering structures of possibility, but the possibilities offered by these works in particular include the transformation of the nation, and even define the nation in terms of its capacity for such transformation. Depicting (and addressing) people who are blind to, deluded about, or unaware of the larger story to which they contribute no more than a microscopic and perhaps unrepresentative part, these works in effect urge their audiences to attune themselves to a deeper rhythm that regulates, or fails to regulate, social and cultural life.

Historical change is never linear or uniform, and the kind of progress to which these works contribute comes with a heavy cost. These works all depict the passing of certain phases or forms of black culture—the Reconstruction period of political assertion, the dreamtime of the river, the Golden Age of the Gullah culture of South Carolina—which are, respectively, destroyed, forgotten, or diluted beyond recognition. The same is true for the white cultures represented in these works, which are shown achieving, respectively, paradise at gunpoint, prosperous and entitled vacuity, and nothing of interest. None of these works seems capable of picturing a society in which cultural differences coexist with equality of opportunity in a rich, sustaining, robust society.

These foundational works do not, then, show American culture at its best. In fact, each contains disturbing or even horrifying scenes that represent some of the most destructive tendencies in American culture, and some of the worst atrocities in American history. But they all issue from and depict a society engaged in ceaseless and often painful self-interrogation, self-discovery, and self-invention, with each resting point, each moment of narrative closure, containing, and failing to contain, the seed of disunion that will impel further change. They all, in their ways, imply that disunion is itself the seed rather than the enemy of progress. The instability resulting from disunion turns out to be the principle of fertility and invention of which many Americans are so proud, as well as the principle of inequality and injustice of which Americans are often ashamed. That paradox is elaborated not in theory but in practice, which is why it fell, at this time and place, to art, and to new forms of mass entertainment in particular, to render it in terms large numbers of people could understand. The genius of America is to begin, in a spirit of naïve confidence and optimism, a heroic obliviousness to obstacles and impediments, the search for a more perfect union; the challenge of America is to admit the necessity of beginning again—and again—to make right what the previous beginning got wrong.

Index